MW00648808

WOMENSCAPE

Selected Stories of Eclectic Women

Susan Helene

Susan Helene

WOMENSCAPE: Selected Stories of Eclectic Women
Copyright © 2022 Susan Helene Nack
All Rights Reserved.
Published by Unsolicited Press.
Printed in the United States of America.
First Edition.

No part of this book may be used or reproduced in any manner
whatsoever without written permission except in the case of brief
quotations embodied in critical articles or reviews.

Attention schools and businesses: for discounted copies on large orders,
please contact the publisher directly.

For information contact:
Unsolicited Press
Portland, Oregon
www.unsolicitedpress.com
orders@unsolicitedpress.com
619-354-8005

Cover Design: Kathryn Gerhhardt
Editor: Robin Lee Ann

ISBN: 978-1-956692-45-7

For Hana, Jaime, and Adina

Acknowledgments

An essential part of this process was the many family members and friends who read, critiqued, and encouraged my writing. Thank you to my readers who took the time to read and comment on my stories: Lynne Horn, Myron Nack, Anne Wolf, Kedma Cantor, Janis Simon, Sharon Muro, Jan Constad, and Rosa, Amelia, and Sara Diaz. Your friendship and willingness to help are greatly appreciated. Thank you to Jaime Nack, my personal web consultant, who patiently guided me through many technical details.

I want to thank the Long Beach California RAG Writers group for their comments, criticism, and encouragement and Laura Perkins, my editor, whose thoughtful review of the manuscript was invaluable. I am also grateful for the information gleaned from the lectures of Marla Miller and Jennifer Silva Redmond at the Southern California Writers' Conference.

There are many other friends who also enrich my life. Thank you, Nancy Mahoney, Chantal Joubert-Honecki, Sharon Muro and Joanne Feldman for your friendship. Thank you to my PFF friends—you know who you are—for coming back into my life with open hearts. My life has been enriched even further by my daughters, Adina and Jaime, and my granddaughter, Hana. They are each talented in ways unique to themselves. More importantly, they are good, caring women and my best friends.

A special thank you to my niece, Jennifer Wolf Kam, a talented author of young adult novels, for her help and to my parents, George and Sally Schneider. My mother for gifting her dry wit and humor to me, and my father for instilling in me his love of books and respect for the writing craft.

Finally, thank you Unsolicited Press for believing in this work.

Contents

In the Beginning...   9

Affirmations   17

Rachel's Tomb   24

Venus Rising   35

Feat of Clay   51

Diana, The Huntress   55

Oedipus Wrecks   64

Resurrection   79

Her Cup Runneth Over   100

Revival   108

Samson and Delilah   115

A Time to Live, A Time to Die   125

In the Beginning...

In her short life of five years, Lily Ann Merchant was very sure of one thing—she was exceptionally beautiful. She had noticed this from the time she could sit up in her stroller. Trips to the park and rides in the supermarket cart produced a parade of admirers bending down to give homage. Her curly auburn hair and peaches-and-cream complexion set off by large, gray-green eyes framed by thick, dark eyelashes produced an array of positive reactions:

"Such a cutie!"

"What gorgeous hair!"

"See how it frames her face and those red lips—such a doll!"

"Look at those eyes and those eyelashes!"

"I could eat her up!"

(This last one initially frightened Lily Ann. She soon discovered, however, that the threat was idle; the admiration was real.)

Lily Ann and her mother never held hands. Her mother, a wannabe beauty queen with an expanding girth, propelled Lily Ann ahead of her with a firm hand on her shoulder. Lily

Ann assumed that was her mother's way of saying, "Look at what I made."

Lily Ann learned early how to play to her audience: smile when they smiled, giggle when they talked baby talk, and bat those big eyes with a sidelong glance to attract even more attention. In short, she knew her beauty was her weapon, and she employed it with great aplomb.

She used it to manipulate her peers in preschool, who were not immune to her wiles. A special smile from Lily Ann and a favored toy would be relinquished, a seat vacated at the lunch table, or a cookie shared. Her teachers were easily swayed by a wishful glance or a soft-spoken request. It was rare to see another seated on the teacher's lap during story time. Lily Ann ruled. The first day of kindergarten, therefore, brought with it no anxiety for her.

Lily Ann had geared up to make her usual great first impression. She had insisted on her green party dress with pink roses embroidered on the hem and collar, because she knew the green set off her eyes. Her confidence was reinforced as she walked up the long, straight path leading to the kindergarten/first grade wing. A shy smile here and a sideward glance there produced the desired admiration

"You have a new teacher, and I hear she's wonderful," her mother declared. "Her name is Ms. Fischer. Your classroom is number six, just around this corner."

Lily Ann was not fully paying attention. Turning the corner, she noticed a strange occurrence. The children and parents coming toward her were acting very odd. Instead of directing admiring glances at her, they were looking back over their shoulders and whispering to each other with great enthusiasm.

She looked ahead. Standing outside room six, facing away from her, was a tall woman with jet black hair. The woman was talking with another woman of stocky build who was stroking the head of a similarly short boy. It was the look on the boy's face that was disconcerting. It was a look of awe. It was a look Lily Ann was familiar with; she had seen it before. It was a look, Lily Ann had always assumed, that only she could inspire.

The mother gently pushed her son into the classroom, said a few words to the teacher, and walked toward Lily Ann and her mother. Lily Ann smiled at the passing mother, who smiled briefly, looked back one more time, and walked by. Lily Ann's head whipped around just as Ms. Fischer turned to greet Lily Ann and her mother.

Lily Ann froze in her steps. Before her stood a vision of loveliness. Ms. Fischer's black hair was swept away from her face into a chignon. Large blue eyes rimmed with dark eyelashes looked at Lily Ann with intense interest. Her smile revealed beautiful white teeth framed by a full, welcoming mouth. As Lily Ann's mother and Ms. Fischer exchanged greetings, Lily Ann stood frozen. With grace and purpose, Ms. Fischer stooped down to Lily Ann's level to greet her.

Ms. Fischer's mouth moved, yet Lily Ann heard nothing. She nodded dumbly at Ms. Fischer. It was not that she didn't hear exactly. It was that her mind was in a turmoil. She was slowly coming to the realization that kindergarten might be a challenge. She had seen Ms. Fischer's effect on that boy. There was no way she could use her tried-and-true techniques on a classroom of kids who were under Ms. Fischer's spell. Ms. Fischer had authority, adulthood, and (let's face it) gorgeousness. Would Lily Ann's adorableness be able to compete?

Her mother spoke to her and gave her a gentle shove into the classroom. Because she was one of the last to enter—a purposeful move on Lily Ann's part to make a grand entrance—the only chair left was at a table in the back of the room. The sniveling boy she had seen at the door and a tall, gangly girl with red hair and candy-striped glasses occupied two of the four seats. No way was she going to sit there!

Scanning the classroom, she saw one boy looking at her. Perceiving this as an opening, she tilted her head to one side and put on a pitiful, yet appealing, look.

"Could I sit here, please?" Lily Ann softly asked.

He looked around, began to get up, and then stopped.

"You're fine right there, Timothy. Thanks for being such a gentleman." Ms. Fischer's melodic voice wafted from behind Lily Ann. Turning to Lily Ann, she continued, pressing a hand on Lily Ann's back, and guiding her toward the back of the room. "Why don't you come sit here with Michelle and Rory?" Her gentle but firm hand guided Lily Ann into one of the empty seats.

This would not do. Lily Ann NEVER sat in the back of any class. She glanced up at Ms. Fischer with one of her oh-so-cute, plaintive looks—but to no avail.

"You'll have a turn to sit up front. We take turns here in kindergarten."

Turns? Lily Ann did not wait for her turn, ever! She tried to look pleasant and endearing as she took her seat, but the effort was too much for her. Her smile was more of a grimace. Rory and Michelle seemed to shrink away from her. She was alarmed. This feeling of rejection was new and unwelcomed. She would win. She would regain control of herself and Ms. Fischer. She watched and waited.

For a kindergarten class, it was very quiet. All eyes were on Ms. Fischer when she talked. All instructions she delivered were followed without complaint. When the class went to the activity centers lined up under the windows, the students talked in low, reverential tones. Ms. Fischer circulated among the stations, offering guidance, answering questions, and giving praise and encouragement. Lily Ann soon found that her charms worked on the small scale of the activity centers. That was until Ms. Fischer noticed her maneuverings and intervened.

"Lily Ann, let's let Billy finish the dinosaur puzzle. After he's done, you may have a turn with it. Why don't you work on this teddy bear puzzle for now?"

"Melissa picked out that hat to wear. Can you find another one, Lily Ann?"

"Sean is using the red shovel now. Here's a blue shovel for you, Lily Ann."

Storytime was a huge disappointment. A large, circular mat, decorated around the rim with animal pictures, was laid out in front of an adult sized wooden chair. Ms. Fischer instructed the children to choose an animal to sit upon. Lily Ann wanted the elephant, but Rory beat her to it, plopping down upon the poor creature with great joy. She started toward Rory, determined to charm her way onto the pachyderm's spot. A look of defiance from Rory discouraged her. Looking around, she saw the choice places next to the teacher's chair were occupied. Trying to look nonplussed, she daintily walked across the rug and sat on the remaining picture. It was a pig.

Lily Ann was not pleased.

Snack time followed. Each child received a carton of milk and three slices of apple. Lily Ann was dismayed to see the skin had been left on the fruit. She tried to peel it off with her teeth. She stopped when she noticed two of the girls exchanging glances and giggling. Screwing up her face and with great determination, she chomped down on the unappealing apple. She had to admit, although the skin felt weird in her mouth, the fruit was quite nice. She gave a smile of satisfaction and was surprised when one of the girls smiled back.

Had any child ever smiled at her before? If she was honest, the answer was not really. The girl screwed up her face, took a bite in turn, and laughed. Lily Ann opened her mouth wide and chomped down on her apple with gusto. The girl did the same. Lily Ann laughed. A new sensation. It was a real laugh that emanated from her—not a contrived one. They proceeded to alternate bites of their apples, giggling. As Lily Ann stood in line to throw away her milk carton, she felt a tap on her shoulder. She turned to see the laughing girl.

"I'm Christina. What's your name?"

"Lily Ann."

"You're very pretty."

Lily Ann looked at Christina with a discerning eye. She had dark brown eyes, copper skin, and wavy, black hair, which she wore in two pigtails. Lily Ann didn't know quite what to say. She realized another child had never approach her on equal footing. She was always either admired or feared. She knew she should say something, so she said the first thing that came into her head.

"You're very funny."

Christina giggled. Lily Ann giggled.

Christina was very good at putting together puzzles. Sitting at the puzzle table, they swapped puzzles, and when Ms. Fischer gave them a "special" puzzle with twenty-five pieces, they worked together harmoniously. This was a new situation for Lily Ann. Although awkward at first, she found herself letting Christina take the lead, passing puzzle pieces to her when Lily Ann was stumped. This continued until Ms. Fischer asked the children to clean up and get ready to go home.

"Christina? Lily Ann? Could you stay a bit and finish up the puzzles on the puzzle station?"

Lily Ann frowned. It wasn't her job to finish someone else's puzzle.

Ms. Fischer, seeing Lily Ann's negative reaction, decided to try another tactic. "You girls are my best puzzle solvers. I think I shall call you our Puzzle Masters!"

"We're the Puzzle Masters!" Christina exclaimed, turning to Lily Ann. "Gimme a high five!"

Lily Ann had seen this done before but had never been invited to do it. She tentatively raised her hand, and Christina high fived her. Clasping Lily Ann's hand, she pulled her to the puzzle table, and they set to work. The Puzzle Masters finished in no time.

Ms. Fischer busily helped the other students put on their coats and gather their belongings, glancing every so often at the two girls working so well together.

As they put on their coats, Christina chatted, and Lily Ann mostly listened. This, also, was new to her. She rarely talked to other kids, let alone listened. Ms. Fischer followed her class out to the pickup zone. Christina and Lily Ann were the last to leave.

Christina waved to a larger version of herself, who was balancing a baby on one hip with one hand and waving with the other. "There's my mom. See you tomorrow!"

"Mine too. See ya!" Lily Ann shouted after her. Sensing Ms. Fischer behind her, she turned and gave a tentative smile.

Ms. Fischer smiled back and watched Lily Ann run toward her mother. As she walked back into the building to the appreciative glances of others, Ms. Fischer turned, catching her reflection in the glass doors.

She smiled. Still got it.

Affirmations

Melissa stared at herself in the mirror and did not like what she saw. "I am strong. I am smart. I am capable. I am kind. I am..."

Melissa's mother stood in the doorway—tall, thin, and lovely. Her reflection seemed to mock Melissa's own. "Go on, Melissa. Finish the affirmation."

Her mother strode into the room and, reaching from behind, swept Melissa's hair up into her perfectly manicured hands.

"Finish, please!" She reached for the hairbrush on the end table and began to guide it through Melissa's hair.

Melissa suppressed a sigh. "I am beautiful."

"And so, you are." Her mother reached for the red scrunchie. "I think you look adorable today! Perfect for the fourth-grade holiday assembly. I do wish you'd gotten the smaller sweatshirt though. Look how long it is—almost to your knees."

Melissa's eyes drifted down. She had not wanted to buy the red leggings. Her mother insisted that if she wanted the snowman sweatshirt, she would need the leggings. So, she had fought for the girls' size XL sweatshirt. It flowed over her protruding belly and hid her thighs. She desperately wanted the snowman sweatshirt. The fuzzy white snowman would, she hoped, serve as a distraction from the body underneath. Perfect for the assembly. For once, she might fit in.

Melissa came into the kitchen, her mother's arm around her shoulder in a reassuring hug.

Her father applauded her holiday look. "Ho, Ho, Ho! You look great! You will shine on that stage today. Just so you know, young lady, I'm taking my lunch late, so I can come and watch. So, sing loud for your Daddy."

Melissa felt a pang of panic. The singing didn't bother her. It was the dancing routine where she felt the most uncomfortable. It was just hand motions and tiny steps on the risers, but she felt self-conscious nevertheless. She was not only the tallest in the class; she was the fattest. Her stomach seemed to jiggle with every move, no matter how small. She was grateful that her teacher had placed her in the back row.

She sat on the school bus, alone as usual. She no longer attempted to share a seat, and no one asked to sit next to her for fear of Elena and Lisette's wrath. They were the "popular" girls, although no one really liked them. They were pretty, and they were mean. They had spent the first week of school targeting Melissa and anyone else who dared to share her seat on the bus.

"Careful! She'll squash you."

"You don't want to sit there. Fat people smell."

"I'd find another seat if I were you. You don't want people to think you like her."

Melissa's defense was to stare out the window and avoid eye contact with anyone, especially those two.

Today, it didn't work.

Lisette started it. "Love the snowman. Is that a relative? You kinda look alike."

Elena agreed. "Gotta be! Look at his tummy. I bet if you turned sideways, your stomach would be as round as his. Go ahead. Stand up. Come on, everyone. Tell her to stand up."

Lisette took up the chant, raising her hands like a conductor. "Stand up! Stand up!"

Everyone turned to look. Melissa sought out a friendly face, but, as usual, there wasn't one. A few joined in the chant. Some had sheepish grins. Most, thankfully, glanced at her and then quickly turned back, embarrassed.

The bus driver jerked the bus to a stop and glared at Lisette. "Sit down, Lisette, and be quiet. Or I'll report you to the assistant principal."

Lisette gave a gratuitous curtsy and plopped down.

When the bus trip ended, Melissa bolted for the sanctuary of the girls' room, holding back tears as she stared at the mirror. The sterile white tile walls and dull gray stall doors stood in stark contrast to her reddened face. She banged on the faucet, ripped a paper towel off, dampened it, and placed it over her eyes. She heard the bathroom door swing open. She stiffened.

"Well, if it isn't little Miss Snow Girl. Don't cry too hard. Your tears might melt you."

Melissa slowly lowered the paper towel. In the mirror's reflection, she saw Lisette and Elena standing behind her, grinning conspiratorially. Had they followed her in?

Elena nudged Lisette who turned to Melissa. "Don't worry, Melissa. You'd have to cry all day before you could melt away."

"I'm not crying. I'm just hot!"

The two girls snickered.

A small, firm voice interrupted. "Why should she be crying? She looks way cooler than you with your *so* predictable yoga pants and too-tight T-shirts." Standing in the open door of the last stall, arms crossed in defiance, was a very small, very thin girl.

"Who the heck are YOU, Peewee?"

The girl eyed Elena with disdain. "I'm her friend. That's who, Miss Yoga Pants."

"Her friend? Nobody's HER friend."

Lisette tapped Elena on the shoulder, and the two girls turned to leave.

The small girl was not done. "Well, that's too bad. They don't know what they're missing."

The bathroom door swung closed.

Melissa stared at this unusual girl. "Why did you do that?"

The girl shrugged. "I meant it. You do look cool."

20

"No, I don't. I'm too fat."

"I'm too thin."

A smile passed between them. The tiny girl walked to the bank of sinks. She strained on her tippy toes to reach the faucet.

Melissa reached over and turned on the cold water.

"Thanks."

"Thank you too. I'm Melissa. I don't think I've seen you at school before. Are you new?"

"I'm Anna. No. I've been here all along. I'm in Ms. Hardwick's class, but I sit way in the back, away from everyone. And I come in late and leave early."

Melissa was puzzled. "How come?"

"I have brittle bone disease. That means that my bones break easily. My parents are a bit paranoid about it. I avoid crowds, so I don't get bumped."

Melissa had broken a finger once and remembered how painful it had been. "Have you ever broken any bones?"

Anna nodded. "When I was in preschool, the school called Child Protective Services because I came to school with a broken arm twice. They thought my parents were abusing me. That's when they found out I had the disease. I don't have a bad case. Some people can hardly be touched. I need a good bump or fall to break a bone. The bummer is that my parents are afraid to hug me. I would really like a hug sometimes."

21

"That sucks." Melissa thought of her mother's arms encompassing her that morning. "Does that mean you won't be in the holiday assembly?"

Anna feigned a look of shock, her hands flying up to her cheeks in mock horror. "Oh, heavens no! Risers crammed with children? Think of all the dangerous possibilities. No, I get to watch from the projection booth with the secretary, Ms. Chatsworth. It's the best seat in the house."

Melissa decided to take a leap of faith. "Would you like to come over and play sometime?"

Anna's expression said it all. "My mom won't allow it. She's afraid something will happen, and I'll end up in the hospital again. People who have this sometimes end up in a wheelchair because they've broken too many bones, and their bones become too weak to support them. The doctor says that it probably won't happen to me, but just try and convince my mom."

The girls stood awkwardly.

Anna broke the silence. "Do you have a phone? We could text each other. Maybe call sometimes?"

Melissa beamed. Anna took a pink phone from her sweater pocket. Melissa hurriedly unzipped her backpack and pulled out an almost identical pink phone.

As the girls typed their numbers into each other's phones, Anna declared, "You're the first friend in my new phone."

Melissa smiled. Anna would be her first friend too—her only friend since she had started at this new school. The girls returned each other's phones just as the first bell rang.

"Gotta go now. Look for me in the projection booth. You should be able to see my shadow. I'll wave." Anna grabbed her small backpack off the stall hook and hurried out the door.

Melissa picked her backpack off the floor, threw out the wet paper towel, and walked slowly out into the hallway.

Lisette and Elena mockingly rubbed their stomachs as she walked past them.

Melissa smiled. Her thoughts were elsewhere.

I am strong. I am smart. I am capable. I am kind, and…I have a FRIEND!

Rachel's Tomb

"We need to talk to you and your brother tonight," Rachel's mother tentatively announced when Rachel flounced in from school and dropped her backpack smack in the middle of the foyer.

Rachel had seen it coming. Being the savvy twelve-year-old she was, she knew all the signs of divorce. She had seen it first in her friends' homes—the bickering, the blaming, the fits of silence between the parents, the heated, whispered arguments in the bedroom.

She read the signs right; she was sure of it. Late night conversations behind closed doors with low voices tinged with urgency and disagreement. Tense dinners with vacuous small talk and furtive glances exchanged between her parents.

Her little brother, Matthew, was not oblivious to it either. At six, he was a real baby. As the only boy cousin in their extended family, he was used to being catered to and pampered. His mother's current distracted air made him even clingier than before. Even though his parents had kept him out of school for an extra year, he still seemed to have trouble adjusting to kindergarten. For the past three weeks, he had come home with small bruises on his arms and neck.

His parents had been called to the school numerous times. There had been whispered phone calls between her mother and the school psychologist, Dr. Graef.

The phone started ringing, and Rachel picked it up. She knew who it was as soon as he said hello. She had spent enough time talking with the good old doc to recognize the voice.

"It's Dr. Graef, the school psycho doc," Rachel called to her mother who, rushing up from the basement with laundry, swiped the portable phone out of her hand as if it'd been a forbidden cigarette and retreated to the basement.

Rachel cracked the basement door open, thinking the conversation was about her but was gladdened to hear Matthew's name mentioned. The little prince was having mental problems. Matthew was a wuss.

Not Rachel. She was the rebel. It was not uncommon for her antics to cause dismay and disappointment to her parents. She was an "underachiever" and "behaviorally challenged,"according to her teachers. It had become rare for one of her report cards to come home without the box titled "Unsatisfactory for Conduct" checked.

Rachel hadn't always been so difficult. Before Matthew came along, she enjoyed being the first grandchild. As the eldest granddaughter, she enjoyed a few years of unabated attention. As new girl cousins arrived, Rachel ruled family gatherings with fairness and wisdom that the oldest should possess. Matthew's birth had dethroned her somewhat. Still, she spared the little prince from her direct wrath. She acted as the wise and caring big sister to Matthew. She was smart enough to know how transparent her jealousy would appear.

So, she turned it inward, tormenting the very parents who thought she was not enough by sabotaging herself. She started first grade with all the promise her parents had foretold, but after Matthew's birth, she become the bane of their existence. The principal knew Rachel well, as did the vice principal who supervised detention and—of course—so did Dr. Graef.

If Rachel was honest, she would admit she had worked hard for this day. She had done everything possible to create havoc within her family. At the very least, divorce would mean separate households. Perhaps she would go and live with her father, since Matthew was still a baby and needed his mommy. She could work the guilt on her father. Maybe she would finally get her own cell phone. If not, well, Dad worked until 6 p.m. most weekdays. There would be plenty of time for unlimited phone chats. Although she was not yet interested in boys, the impending freedom from being home alone was intriguing. Oh yes, Rachel would be the center of attention for poor, deluded Dad.

If she had to stay with her mother, there would be visitation weekends with Dad. She knew how this worked. Many of her friends' parents were divorced, and she had learned a lot from them. She envied the new clothes their guilty fathers bought them. She longed to wear the makeup they wore when returning from their fathers' places— something their mothers would never have allowed. Maybe she could even get a season pass to the new theme park opening up. Oh yes, divorce had dividends, and she was ready to cash in.

She had to play it smart. Creating tears on demand was her specialty; it had gotten her through many jams in the past. Concern and sadness would be the proper mood. She could see it now. Her mother would spout the standard line all parents tell their children when they were getting divorced.

"It's not your fault, Rachel. Your father and I just grew apart."

Her father would follow with the promise of fidelity all fathers make.

"Even though I won't be living here anymore, I won't love you any less. I'm still your dad, and we'll have weekends to spend together."

Dinner began as usual. Except this time, the forced civility was laughable. Rachel always enjoyed the way her parents tiptoed around her. They knew they had to ask about school while also knowing they did not want to hear the answer. She had perfected her technique of feigned nonchalance and—well, yes—a bit of a sociopathic attitude for good measure.

Dad asked the obligatory question. "How was school today, Rachel?"

"Oh, yeah. Forgot to tell you. I've got detention all next week. That witch, Ms. Price, caught me cheating on my spelling test."

Her mother's fork poised in midair then slowly descended back onto her plate. Her pained look was classic. "Oh, Rachel, why would you cheat when you're so smart?"

Rachel decided this tactic would be even more effective with some embellishment. "Because I can." She triumphantly shoveled mashed potatoes into her mouth and proceeded to talk with a full mouth, spewing white flecks of potato onto the glass tabletop. "I cheat all the time. I'm really good at it. This is the first time I got caught, and besides, spelling tests are stupid."

Her father glanced beseechingly at her mother, carefully wiped his mouth with his napkin, and cleared his throat. "Rachel. Your mother and I have been talking a lot lately, and we've made an important decision. We feel it is the right decision for us and for you and Matthew."

Here it is, Rachel thought, almost choking on her mash potatoes. Hmm. That came across well—the choking. Nice touch. She congratulated herself on the unplanned display. It was time to load the ammunition and get ready to fire as needed.

"What decision?" she asked, trying to add a note of confusion to her voice.

"Things haven't been right here for quite a while. A home should be a safe place—a place of love." He glanced uncomfortably at her mother.

Her mother was staring at Rachel and absently stroking Matthew's arm. He shoved his head further into his mother's side. His right arm was wrapped around her waist, and his left arm clutched his right side as if he were physically holding himself together.

I could learn from this kid, Rachel thought. Clinging like that had a nice effect—not too obvious, probably good for a special occasion. Instead, she stayed silent. She didn't want to make this easy for them. This was her moment, and she wanted to savor their discomfort. It seemed like the obvious move. The more discomfort for them, the more goodies for her in the long run. She furrowed her brow in feigned confusion.

"What Dad is trying to say is that we feel, at least for a while, that we need to take some time apart."

Bingo! I'm in. Rachel thought. Let the tears flow. "Do you mean you're getting a divorce?" she cried out in poignant anguish, turning tear-filled eyes toward her father. All her practice was paying off big time. She was really into this now. Maybe she'd join the drama club next year. She could see her parents sitting on opposite sides of the auditorium, watching her steal the show, with Matthew sitting between them, completely ignored.

Ah! Back on top again! What a turnaround she would stage. From troubled child to class star. How her parents would regret having subjected her to their failed marriage. And how willingly they would buy her forgiveness, making it up to her with gifts and privileges. She was ready for this—so ready.

Bring on the goodies!

Her parents' faces collapsed in grief and shock. Matthew grabbed his mother's waist and started to cry, burying his head even deeper into her side.

Rachel was getting annoyed. *Geez. Lay off the hysterics, kid.*

Matthew wiped nose snot off with his red, striped T-shirt. *Disgusting!*

Her dad's face became calm and composed. Speaking in a measured tone, he placed a hand on her shoulder and gave it a gentle squeeze. "Rachel. I'm so sorry. We didn't mean to upset you. Your mother and I love each other. We're not getting a divorce."

Rachel couldn't believe it. What were they thinking? Of course, they were getting a divorce, and she was going to get everything she wanted, whenever she wanted. What kind of crap was this? What exactly did they mean by "taking time apart"?

"I don't understand." She tried to convert her inner rage into outward confusion. She glanced from one parent to the other. Her hands shot up and covered her mouth as if to stifle the moan which unexpectedly rose from within her.

Maybe they meant a "trial separation." *Hold on girl,* she admonished herself. *All is not lost. Don't blow this.*

"Well, Rachel." Her mother responded in that "mommy" voice that drove her crazy. "Your father and I have found you a lovely boarding school in Connecticut. It's an all-girls school, and they have small classes and counseling. You know, someone to talk to about—well—about anything bothering you. You could still come home on holidays to be with us, and…"

Rachel stopped listening. She needed to think. This was not the plan. What happened to the "it's-not-your-fault" speech? Get rid of Rachel, and Mom, Dad, and Matthew could live happily ever after? She needed a new plan of action. She needed to turn this around and fast!

"You hate me! You love Matthew, and you hate me!" She flung her father's hand off her shoulder and slouched down in her chair, crossing her arms.

Matthew stopped weeping and stared dazedly at Rachel. Clinging to his mother's side, he choked back sobs. His dismayed mother bent over, muttered consoling sounds, and stroked his back as if petting a cat.

"Rachel." Her father's tone was firm.

Rachel was starting to get scared.

"We know you've been hurting Matthew. Do you think we didn't see the marks you left on his arms and neck? We can't let you go on hurting him and…" He paused for effect. "Hurting yourself."

What the hell was going on? Rachel was losing it. She stood up abruptly and pushed her chair so violently that it fell over. Its wooden legs screeched over the oak floor. "What are you talking about? I never touched Matthew. He's lying!"

"Now, Rachel." That "mommy voice" again. "Matthew didn't tell us. The school called us in. They were going to investigate us for child abuse. Dr. Graef finally got Matthew to tell her. You've been pinching him and threatening to beat him up if he told on you. We love you, Rachel. But you need help. That's why we're sending you to Waverly School. They have wonderful counselors there."

Rachel looked at her mother, then her father, and then Matthew. His hand moved under the shirtsleeve of his arm. Slowly, the fabric of the shirt moved upward, exposing his thumb and forefinger drawing together, a bulge of reddening skin emerging from the ever-closing gap between his fingers.

The little rat was pinching himself! Rachel glared at him.

He smiled a slow, ever-so-tiny smile. His eyes, normally a pale green, seemed to glimmer with an unnatural light.

"He's doing it to himself. Look!"

Matthew turned his face into his mother's side. He began to weep. Her parents exchanged sad and knowing glances.

Rachel's parents didn't even bother to drive her there themselves. A black sedan with the school logo—complete with a chaperone, an ugly, old woman—pulled up the drive the following Monday. Her parents kissed and hugged her. Rachel stood stoically, showing no reaction to their affection. She would not let them see her crack.

The chaperone grabbed Rachel's arm with a firm grip, leaving Rachel to muse as to whether this was an old woman or an old man. Her parents stayed on the porch while Matthew ran down the walk and waited at the side of the car, looking confused and bereft.

Rachel broke free of the woman's grip and walked straight to the car. She let herself into the back seat, disregarding Matthew's presence. She rolled down the window to try to escape the musty smell of the sedan and the insipid rose water scent of the chaperone's perfume.

Standing at the car window, looking all innocent and sweet, was little Matthew.

The chaperone, sitting in the front seat, turned to watch.

"I love you, Rachel. Why did you have to hurt me?" he proclaimed in his small, weepy voice.

"It's all right, little man. She loves you too, and she's so sorry. Aren't you Rachel?"

Rachel glared at the chaperone, saying nothing.

The chaperone turned around in disgust and started the car. "You have a lot to learn, Missy, picking on a sweet boy like your brother. And I am an excellent teacher. Believe me!" The chaperone hissed as she shifted the car into drive.

Rachel turned to glare at her brother then stopped. He held her stare with his. That glimmer was in his eyes again. She could feel the fear building inside her. The black sedan moved forward down the drive. Matthew turned and ran up the walk into his mother's arms.

The last thing Rachel remembered of that day was her parents standing on the porch, waving sadly after the car, while Matthew stood in front of them, feet in a wide stance, waving and grinning. Grinning and waving.

Rachel's parents visited at Christmas. She wasn't allowed to come home; her behavior at school warranted this punishment. Her parents, however, tried to cheer her up with news from home.

Her mother's cheerful expression had a tinge of fear around her eyes. "Matthew wanted to come. We thought you'd like to know he's doing so well at school. The teachers say he is quite the performer. Got the lead in the Christmas play. We are so proud. He did such a good job."

Now, it was her father's turn. "We thought it best for Matthew not to come today. We thought he deserved a reward for doing so well this fall. So, he's going with Aunt Sharon's family to that new theme park. It just opened."

Venus Rising

Venus Goldfarb awoke to absolute silence and the sunlight seeping through the Venetian blinds. She glanced at the faded pink Cinderella clock on the battered furniture. Ten o'clock. She remembered. It was Labor Day weekend; her parents must be on their annual pilgrimage to the Catskills. Lazily, she traced the lines of light on the opposing wall. No need to get up. No need to move. No one to nudge her out of her comfy bed. No nagging. She was so tired of their nagging. So tired of their mournful looks of disappointment. Today, she would relish the solitude, the peace.

She stretched, her hands reaching over the headboard and her feet peeking out from beneath her quilt. She had nowhere to go and nothing she had to do, and that was how she liked it.

Venus felt cursed from birth. She was the only daughter of elderly parents. Her father, Sol, named her after the famous painting by Botticelli, *The Birth of Venus*. A copy of the painting—Venus, naked and coy, rising from an oversized clamshell—graced the front foyer. It had been the source of embarrassment for Venus from childhood. She learned early to never invite friends to her house, especially if her father was home.

"Come, child," Sol would say, escorting the unfortunate victim to the foyer. "Let me show you Venus' namesake."

He would launch into a long discourse on the merits of the painting and the powers of Venus, as the hapless, blushing child politely averted her eyes.

"Our Venus!" Sol would proclaim, patting Venus on her bowed head. "She will be someday just like this Venus—a beauty!"

Got that one wrong, Sol!

Sol, however, was never wrong, and of Venus' beauty, he was certain. To Sol, she was his mother incarnate— beautiful and saintly. Venus had once seen an old daguerreotype of her grandmother. She was seated on an overstuffed settee, her short arms barely clasping each other over an ample stomach. Her three sons adoringly arranged about her—Sol, the youngest, straining to rest his little hand on her shoulder. She had a round, unremarkable face, which smiled beatifically from under a too-small wide brim hat. If this was Sol's vision of beauty, then Venus was beautiful all right. Unfortunately, four years of high school without a single date convinced her that his idea of beauty was unique to himself.

Yesterday had been the day of all days for guilt. Her parents had broken the unspoken rule; they had brought up her future.

"Venus, darling," her mother, Esther, began. And there it was, the famous "Venus darling" opener, a sure sign of a forthcoming guilt trip. "Your Aunt Naomi tells me her Sharon is going to start classes at that school they've been advertising on TV. She's going to be a dental hygienist. You know, your teeth are so much nicer than Sharon's. You should look into that school. You'd be hired by any dentist, what with your beautiful smile." Her mother looked less than convinced by her own words.

Venus let her tongue slide over her perfect teeth. It was a nice try. This was not a new approach—playing on her imagined strengths. When everyone else was schlepping their kids to the orthodontist, Sol and Esther would brag about how their daughter had no need for braces.

"Surely," Esther would often proclaim, "no dentist would reject a patient (and give up the money) unless they had no choice." Ergo, Venus had to have "perfect teeth".

Aunt Naomi, who resided in an adult living community in Florida, was constantly prodding Esther to be more assertive with Venus.

Esther was giving it her best. "It's been almost three months since you graduated." Her voice wavered. She knew she was treading on dangerous ground. "You're such a talented girl, Venus. Remember those wonderful sock puppets you made in the third grade? And you have a flair for design. The way you arranged all those posters on your wall with each one slightly off from the next. It's so original. And..." Her mother prattled on.

Venus groaned as she forced her mother's voice to fade into the background. She had bought those posters of rock groups to try to fit in with her peers. And they were crooked because she hadn't cared enough to spend the time lining them up. Those were now several years old. She stopped buying posters when she stopped having friends over. After all, how could she fit in if no one was there to witness her conformity?

The reality was that Venus hated rock, rap, and any of the music she was supposed to love. She liked showtunes, though she knew it wasn't cool. Her favorite was *West Side Story*. Despite her light brown hair and fair, freckled face, she identified with Maria, played by Natalie Wood—small, sultry in an innocent way, and so beautiful. That was who she would have been, but God had played a trick on her and given her Sol and Esther for parents, along with a squat, fat Grandmother whose eyes were too close together.

"Mom, I don't want to stare into gaping mouths all day, and the last thing I want to do is hang up other people's posters," she replied in frustration.

"My darling, Venus," Sol chided. "We're only concerned for your future. What do you want to do? You know, we won't be around forever."

"Well, right now, I'm focused on decompressing from high school. So, leave me alone!" She had theatrically flounced back to her bedroom, slammed the door, and waited until her parents left to "pick up a few things," as they did every day. She would then sprint for the kitchen and wolf down her standard breakfast of chocolate milk and Hostess cupcakes. Her parents once tried to deny her the cupcakes, but the wrath of Venus sent Esther back to the store for a twelve pack.

She returned to her room and spent the whole day in bed listening to WTUN—the only station playing nonstop Broadway tunes. She heard her parents moving around the apartment, opening and shutting cabinets and drawers, and whispering for the rest of the day.

Don't want to disturb their darling daughter. Venus smiled to herself. Her mother even brought in a lunch and dinner tray to appease her. She watched her mother gingerly place the tray on her end table and said nothing. She thought she saw beads of sweat on Esther's pale brow. Venus felt triumphant. She had never had such an effect on her parents. They were afraid of her! That evening, to drive home the point, she never ventured out of her bedroom—the ultimate silent treatment. She was really getting good at this game.

Venus rolled over and listened to the silence. The growling of her stomach stirred her to action, so she rolled out of bed and shuffled to the door.

They were gone. Not just gone out—gone.

The little dog statuettes that once cluttered every horizontal surface were gone. The front hall closet stood empty. Her brown trench coat was the lone occupant, hanging cockeyed, just as she had left it.

She approached her parents' bedroom. This was a place she normally avoided at all costs. The room always had an old smell. It was a mix of her father's Old Spice and her mother's Bengay. It reminded her of the old folks' homes that her mother used to make her visit when she was young and controllable. Shriveled maiden aunts and an elderly gentleman—who Esther claimed was grandmother's cousin—would reach out to touch her cheek and pat her head. Venus was sure her teen acne stemmed from the cooties in those caresses.

The drawers and closets were open and empty like the elderly relatives' empty, gaping mouths. They seemed to be laughing. She backed out of the room into the hallway.

Botticelli had flown the coop.

A faded rectangular shadow gaped back at her. This could only mean one thing. Venus raced to the kitchen.

On the table was a note taped to a jumbo-sized box (twenty count) of hostess cupcakes next to a jar of Ovaltine. She recognized her father's meticulous handwriting.

My dearest Venus,

Your mother and I are off to Florida. We're staying with Aunt Naomi until we sign the papers for our condominium on Tuesday. It's the same over fifty-five development she lives in. You know we always wanted to live in the warm sunshine. We've had enough of New York winters!

We were hoping you would have a job by now and be on your own. Sorry darling, but we are getting older, and the time to move is before you're too old to enjoy it. The rent is paid through the end of the month, and there's

$100 to help with expenses. Your mother and I are confident you will be very successful!

Love,

Your Mother and Father

P.S. Maybe you'll come for a visit this winter?

She didn't know whether to laugh or cry. They had abandoned her! She searched furiously for the one-hundred-dollar bill, finally finding it under the box of cupcakes.

She spoke aloud to the empty apartment. "Okay. Time to take stock. I've got one hundred dollars, a place to stay for the next three weeks, and twenty cupcakes." She opened the refrigerator door. "A gallon of milk, a squeeze bottle of chocolate syrup, some orange juice, some apples, and..." Now the freezer. "Two packages of Nathan's knockwursts and buns."

No need to worry just yet. She grabbed the orange juice and a package of cupcakes and sat down in the wrought iron kitchen chair. She alternated bites of cupcake with swigging orange juice straight from the bottle. This tiny rebellion was empty without her mother's disapproving glare.

Finishing the first package of cupcakes, she pondered whether to have a second. This was a new sensation. She had never hesitated before, but she knew she would have to do her own shopping from now on, and the more she ate, the sooner she'd have to leave the apartment.

Since finishing high school, she rarely ventured outside. To her, "outside" was the breeding ground for disappointment. She had traveled through life shoulders hunched and head down ever since puberty. In one year's time, puberty transformed her from a relatively ordinary girl to an overly wide, awkward creature with unruly hair and overly large breasts. She had no idea how to cope with the stares from men, so she crossed her arms over her chest, hunched her shoulders, and let her hair fall over her face, masking her plain features.

Venus did a visual tour of the apartment. Empty of her parent's things, it at first seemed rather creepy. She found the bare shelves and tabletops disconcerting. Her mother was no interior decorator—and that was an understatement.

Esther had gone through several styles of design, and the remnants of each attempt filled the apartment. Without the unifying theme of Esther's knickknacks, the furniture seemed in total discord. Rattan chairs formed the bookends to an overly upholstered gold velvet couch. A modern, kidney-shaped coffee table in a light, nondescript wood finished the ensemble. The TV—*thank God they had left her that*—was perched on a pressed particle board cart on the other side of the room. A corduroy recliner huddled in the opposite corner. Sol spent his days there, reading the paper, followed by one of the numerous spy novels he adored. The modern, black enamel halogen reading light—a luxury item that cost ninety-nine dollars and ninety-nine cents on sale, according to Sol—still arched over the recliner, as if waiting for him.

Venus plopped down in the recliner. This was a new sensation. She pulled the handle and lurched backward. She always felt it was her father's chair and had never attempted to sit in it, even if he was not home. She felt oddly comfortable sitting in his chair. She, Venus Goldfarb, could sit anywhere she wanted to for the first time in her life; she was not being scrutinized. She was in charge.

In charge of what, she wondered? She was in her parent's apartment, eating food her parents had left her and holding money from her parents. Whereas before they left, she had no qualms about this arrangement, somehow, she felt she needed to take charge of something. Otherwise, there was no point.

So, she decided to take charge of her life and do what she wanted to do, which was to lay in bed, undisturbed, and listen to *The Sound of Music* album. She awkwardly got up from the recliner, slammed the footrest back into place with a sharp kick, and clomped to the bedroom. Leaving her bedroom door wide open for the first time in her life, she snapped the blinds closed and sunk under the familiar pink coverlet. She grabbed her iPhone off her headboard, opened Spotify, and turned the volume up. Clasping her hands behind her back, she closed her eyes as the overture to *The Sound of Music* filled the room.

It did not take long for her to realize the anticipated joy wasn't forthcoming. Her mind kept wandering into the realm of responsibility. She had three weeks rent paid, so she wasn't out on the street yet. She reached into her end table and withdrew her latest bank statement.

She looked at the recently pumped-up balance of three hundred forty-two dollars and sixteen cents. God bless high school graduation. There had been some advantage, at least, of suffering through her senior year of humiliation—no homecoming date, no awards at the awards ceremony, no prom date, and worst of all, an almost pristine yearbook, devoid of good wishes and "in" jokes. In truth, it was almost pristine since Mrs. Snider, the librarian, insisted on signing it. "Best wishes for a wonderful future" she had written as if tacitly admitting the past and present for Venus had been far from wonderful.

In three weeks, she would need four hundred and fifty dollars for rent (ain't rent control wonderful?), and she was almost there. Of course, that meant living off what was in the house for the next three weeks, and that wasn't going to happen. She'd have to earn some money.

She bet her conniving parents had planned that. They must have been planning this for a long time. It suddenly became clear to Venus why, on her eighteenth birthday, her parents signed a new lease and added her name onto it.

"Just in case something happens to us. That way, you won't get thrown out, and they can't raise the rent." Sol solemnly passed the cheap Bic pen to her.

She thought he'd meant in the case of their untimely death, while the whole time he was thinking about a condo in Florida! Suddenly, her parents didn't seem so stupid anymore. They began to take on the aura of crafty conspirators. Venus was pissed, and *The Sound of Music* wasn't doing it for her anymore.

Flipping off the music, she rose and started to dress. Piling her pjs into the corner on top of her worn, brown slippers, she grabbed a black T-shirt off the pile of clean clothes sitting on top of her dresser. Her jeans from yesterday (and the day before) lay crumpled on the floor. They were the pair her mother hated. The hems had been shredded and hung too low on the hip for her ample stomach, and the material sported an appropriately ripped right knee. Esther had been bereft when Venus returned from school with the holey pants.

"Venus! What happened? Those were brand new! Did you fall? Are you all right?"

Venus noticed Esther's concern for the pants came before her concern for her, so she gloried in her response. "I ripped them myself in Geometry class. I finally found a good use for a compass." It was a short step from there to shredding the hems.

Esther had pursed her lips and said nothing.

Venus had found some comfort in her mother's disapproving silence.

She stood before the mirror in her parents' bedroom and decided it was too hot to tuck in the shirt. She ran her fingers through her semi-wavy, semi-curly, non-descript brown hair and stared at her unsatisfactory image. She pulled her unruly bangs down over her left eye. Pocketing the house key and the one-hundred-dollar bill, she left to scope out the neighborhood.

Had Venus been anyone else but herself, she would have noticed it was a beautiful summer day. The temperature was a seasonably cool sixty-four degrees, the sky was clear, and the humidity hovered under thirty percent—a rarity for New York. What she did notice was the inordinately large amount of people on the avenue. Children's laughter from the park across the street echoed off the storefronts; women—strollers rocking absentmindedly at their hips—clustered in groups to window shop and gossip. Worst of all were the couples, old and young, who paraded slowly past her. She watched the dance of courtship. HE, whispering into HER ear. HER head cocked daintily toward HIM—a coy giggle.

Oh, vomit! She shuffled down the sidewalk, dragging the hems of her tattered jeans along the cement. She turned down fifty-first street to escape the crowds on eighth avenue. There were small boutique stores with gold lettering on expansive front windows and cloth canopies in muted colors.

Feeling very out of place, she tried to give the impression that she was urgently heading somewhere. She walked purposely down the street toward what was considered Restaurant Row. She just wanted to get back home to the safety of Sol's chair and the solace of Hebrew National knockwursts. Head down, hands in her pockets, she clung to the storefronts to avoid having to weave in and out of the hordes of shoppers. Every so often, she would glance at a store window, feigning interest in the displays. A Help Wanted sign at Dominic's Italian Bakery and Deli caught her eye.

Maybe she could work in the back, kneading dough, stacking cookies on trays, and slicing bread. If she didn't have to be up front and deal with people, it could work. She considered looking into it tomorrow.

Her mother's voice appeared in her head. *"Venus, you have to dress professionally! No jeans, a nice shirt—maybe the white one with the pretty gold buttons, and the navy skirt you wore to Uncle Marvin's funeral."*

Venus felt the hair on the back of her neck stand up. Her mother hadn't really left, had she? There she was, in her head, telling her what to do.

"Take me as I am or not at all." Venus muttered and headed home.

She wore the white blouse and navy skirt. It irked her to admit that her mother was right. Still, she needed the job. It was the only Help Wanted sign she had seen. She entered Dominic's just after 2 p.m., thinking it would be mostly empty. She was wrong. Apparently, Dominic's was the spot for mothers to catch a cup of coffee and a pastry before school let out. Four old men sat at a round table, placing dominoes between bites of cake and slurping from large mugs. Two men sipped coffee before open laptops. One looked very professional. The other looked very unkempt and kept alternating enthusiastic "yesses" with "damns". Obviously, a gamer and probably unemployed.

The woman behind the counter looked frazzled, taking orders, boxing pastries, and slicing bread. She barely looked at Venus as she handed her an application. Venus sat at an empty table and bent over the paper, hoping to disguise her dismay. Aside from her personal information, she had nothing to write. What chance did she have if she left the experience and references sections blank?

A deep voice boomed from the kitchen. "Gloria! I could use some help back here. These biscotti won't box

47

themselves; you know. I gotta get these breadsticks in the oven if I'm gonna get them to Gina's Trattoria by five."

Gloria glared toward the kitchen, turned back to smile at a waiting customer, slipped a freshly sliced rye bread into a plastic bag, and passed it over the counter to waiting hands. "Hey, you!" she yelled.

Venus looked around. Was Gloria speaking to her?

"Yeah, you. Show me what you got. Go in the kitchen and help that lunk. You do well, and you've got the job."

Venus got up hesitantly. Leaving the mostly blank application on the table, she squeezed past the counter and into the kitchen. It was warm and fragrant. She inhaled deeply. Chocolate chip and oatmeal raisin cookies were cooling on racks. The neglected biscotti were piled on cookie sheets, sorted by type: chocolate, cinnamon, and pistachio. A short, compact man was carefully squeezing yellow flowers onto the layers of a white wedding cake. He smiled weakly and tilted his head toward the rows of ovens behind him.

There stood the largest man Venus had ever seen. His massive hands were grabbing fistfuls of dough and rolling them into thin ropes, which he cut into seven-inch sections. A white bandanna covered his bald head. An apron, that was covered in flour, stretched across an ample stomach. *This must be Dominic.* It was clear that the smaller man decorating the cake would never have earned the title of "lunk."

"Who are you?" The giant glowered at her and turned back to the breadsticks.

48

"I'm the new hire," Venus lied. Though it might soon be true.

"Angelo, show Miss New Hire how to package the biscotti."

The small, wiry man rushed forward. He showed her where the plastic clam shell containers were stacked and handed her a pair of disposable plastic gloves.

"Twelve to a box—like this." He demonstrated, rapidly filling the plastic container. "Be sure to put the right label on the clam shell. Assorted are four of each. Do one of each type and one assorted to make five. Stack them by type on this cart. Got it?"

Venus nodded. The afternoon passed in a blur. Dominic came over once to exam the cart. He grunted and walked away. She, feeling confused, looked to Angelo. For some reason, Angelo's "thumbs up" felt good. She packaged one hundred twenty clam shells of biscotti.

As Gloria brought empty trays back to the kitchen, Venus loaded them anew with cookies, cannoli, and beautiful Italian pastries whose names she struggled to pronounce. It was all she could do not to stick her fingers into the custard fillings or swipe a cookie.

At 6 p.m., the store closed. The staff gathered at the round table for a pastry of their choice and a mug of coffee. Venus liked this perk. She chose a cannoli that oozed cream filling and was coated in milk chocolate. It was heaven on a plate.

"You did well. Didn't she, Dominic?" Gloria asked.

Dominic grunted. He seemed totally absorbed in his cheesecake.

Gloria turned to Venus. "What's your name, hon?"

Venus groaned. How she hated her name. Well, it had to come out sometime. "Venus," she muttered.

Dominic's head shot up. "Venus?" For the first time that day, he was looking at her. There was a smile on his face. "My blessed mother was named Venus."

"Well, I guess that means we have to hire you now," Gloria laughed.

Angelo gave Venus a nod and a wink.

She was in. She was in, not only because she did a good job, but because her name was Venus.

Venus still works at Dominic's, often behind the counter. Her hair is short, and the unruly bangs are gone. She wears a Dominic's red T-shirt and pristine, unripped jeans. Her white apron is spotless, and it's not uncommon to see her smiling.

Esther was right; Venus does have beautiful teeth!

Feat of Clay

Jennifer stared at the array of pottery spread out before her.

Professor Callens put down his mug and slowly shook his head. "You need to find your voice, Jennifer. A senior project makes a statement. Shows direction, an aesthetic. You are all over the place. Look at the other projects around the room." He gave her a pitying look and walked out of the ceramics studio.

He was right, of course. Andy's twelve-place dinner set—not eight but an impressive twelve—had an organic theme. The plates were like cabbage leaves. The mugs and tumblers mimicked the sleek, rounded curves of eggplants. There were Brittany's carved vases, each with the theme of a different flower. Kim's hand-painted tiles formed a hanging quilt with scenes from her childhood on each square.

Jennifer scanned her handiwork. Nothing was fired—a testament to her indecisiveness. Mugs of different shapes and sizes, big bowls, little bowls, round, square, and fluted were stacked in an unstable pile. One large cylinder with no design dominated the collection. She had made it on the wheel just to see if she could throw big. Well, she could throw big all right. Big and boring. She had no idea what to do with it.

Three vases of varying size and shape surrounded the cylinder, dwarfed by its size.

She plopped down onto her stool. There had to be something she could make with what she had. There was no time to start over. Even if she could, she'd have no idea where to start or what to create. Her eyes kept returning to the nondescript cylinder. She moved it out of the collection to stand alone on a turntable. On a whim, she placed the largest vase on top of the cylinder and stood back. She removed the vase, turned it upside down, and put it back. She smiled—that worked. She grabbed another vase and placed it bottom-to-bottom on the first. The last vase was round with a long neck. This she placed on the tower by inserting its neck into the vase below it. She stood back. The tower was about four feet tall. It was going somewhere. She disassembled the tower and reattached the pieces by using slip, a mixture of clay and water.

What the heck could this be? Jennifer searched her mind. She had seen towers like these, but they were more elaborate. What were they called? Suddenly, it came to her. They were totems. She pulled out her phone and went straight to Google. They were used to tell a story. Like Kim's quilt. Jennifer tried to think of a story for her totem. She stared into space. Her family history was boring. Besides, she had no time or inclination to sculpt scenes from her childhood. She would have to tell a story with what lay before her. What story did a collection of mismatched pots tell?

She started with the largest objects, cutting and shaping them to fit the curves of the stacked pottery. As she progressed upward, she first attached the cut-up plates and then the bowls. She stepped back. It needed to be more three-dimensional. She grabbed several mugs of different sizes and cut them crosswise into rings. She lopped off the handles and threaded several rings onto the handles. She attached the ring-filled handles to the totem, separating the rings with small clay balls and securing them with the clay slip. She set about cutting and adhering more pieces of her collection to her totem. The pieces seemed to tell her where they belonged. Her sad collection had been repurposed as unique treasures, and she was finding more and more as she continued to work.

The ball-shaped vase on top gave her an idea. She took two mug bottoms from the pile of dismembered pottery and bored a round hole through each one. She attached them to the center of the round vase on both sides, transforming the vase into a double-sided eyeball.

You want vision, Professor Callens? Here's vision for you. Jennifer picked up a brush and brown iron oxide. She wrote the words of her craft in bold letters and differing fonts and sizes: *wedge, slip, score, sculpt, build, cast, fire, kiln, mold, sgraffito, glaze, trim, tile, cuenca, raku...*

In a final flourish and large flowing letters, she wrote "CLAY" on one side of the base and *"VISION"* on the opposing side.

Jennifer did not hear Professor Callens come into the studio. It was when he circled the totem that she realized that she had company.

"So, Jennifer. Tell me about this...this piece. What's the vision?"

Jennifer looked blankly at the professor. What was she trying to say? "It's a totem."

"I know it's a totem. It has to say something. It can be about history, a story, or a special event. So, which is it?" The sarcasm in her professor's tone was unmistakable.

She sighed. She glanced over at the other students' projects lined up on the counter and then back at her totem. She studied it—trying to look at it objectively. It did tell a story, and it told it well. She knew in her gut that the work was good. "It's the story of my journey in clay. It's also a celebration of the versatility of clay."

The professor's smirk was not comforting. "A celebration? Well, we will see what the Art Department thinks when it's evaluated. I doubt it will be accepted into the Student Show. Good luck."

Jennifer watched his retreating form. Dread welled up inside her. What if this was all a colossal mistake? If her senior project wasn't accepted, she would have no future in art. Her parents would insist she give art up for a more secure profession. She shuddered. Carefully, she moved the totem to the drying shelves. It was done. This was her vision, and she would stand by it.

You can see Jennifer's work today in many renown museums. Her public installations are among the most photographed in the world. Her first totem, "Clay Visions," was chosen by the faculty to be installed in front of the Administration Building. Professor Callens was the one, dissenting vote. But then, art is subjective, isn't it?

Diana, The Huntress

"Will you cut that out?" Tiffany protested in a low, threatening voice, which was barely audible over the noise of the bar. "What do you think you're doing?"

Without taking her eyes off the man across from her at the horseshoe-shaped bar, Diana responded, "Shh! I'm not doing anything!"

However, she was, and she knew it. She was staring hard at this man. She decided tonight would be different. No more furtive glances, hoping for something in return. She was going to be the one in control tonight.

"Yes, you are." Tiffany insisted.

It was easy for Tiffany—going to bars. She was every man's dream. Petite Tiffany with her blonde hair, blue eyes, perky, upturned nose, and perfect posture. She had been a cheerleader (of course) in high school, and ten years later, she looked like she could still wow the crowds into a frenzy. Diana bet Tiffany could still do the splits.

If Diana and Tiffany hadn't reconnected at work six months ago, they would have never been friends. In high school, Diana played basketball and volleyball and felt invisible when she wasn't on the court. She had absolutely been invisible to Tiffany. It surprised her when Tiffany suggested they have lunch together and when it became their daily routine. And it surprised her even more when Tiffany invited her to go to the bar together.

"Well, if you're going to be so obvious, why him? His buddies are cuter."

Why, indeed? Diana thought. She had watched them come in and order beers.

There were three of them. Her mark—*that's it. I'll name him Mark*—was about five feet, ten inches with a pleasant, round face, light brown, slightly thinning hair, and black-rimmed glasses. He was average in build, perhaps ten pounds overweight, and had the look of an accountant. In short, he was what she deserved.

Buddy number one, sitting next to him, had wavy black hair and olive skin—Mediterranean, maybe Arabic or Hispanic. Apart from his short stature, he looked like a Greek god: well-built, perfect hair, perfect white teeth, and—well—just perfect. And he knew it. His eyes surfed the room. He wasn't just looking for a pretty girl but an easy one. Diana was convinced he would find one tonight, and she wasn't even in the running.

Buddy number two looked like a former high school linebacker with an extreme fondness for beer. He carried his large body with the confidence of a man in denial. Handsome enough, he talked a little too loud and gestured a little too large. His black, pullover sweater did little to hide his expanding girth. Still, he projected smoothness and

56

confidence. Tiffany would probably go for him before the night was over.

Buddy number one and Buddy number two scanned the room. Tiffany scanned the room. Mark sat, slowly sipping his beer, and nodded occasionally in response to some comment. Waiting for their eyes to meet, Diana continued her staring vigil. He never seemed to look straight ahead; he looked just to his right, where his buddies were critically assessing the women, assessing the night's potential conquests.

At almost six feet, Diana would be hard to miss. Growing up, she bemoaned her height. She found refuge in basketball and volleyball, where her size and her big, manly hands were assets. She kept her weight down and still ran and played pickup ball at the local YMCA. Still, her broad shoulders made her feel massive. Fortunately, as her mother often pointed out, she had been blessed with decent-sized breasts. Otherwise, Diana was convinced she could easily be mistaken for a man.

Good Lord! How can he miss me?

Her mother had been prescient. Diana, the goddess of the hunt. Aside from giving her an appropriate name, her mother lived in denial. She reveled in Diana's larger than life appearance. She insisted that with Diana's height and her certain look, she could be a model. Although her mother was not into sports herself, she went to every game Diana ever played in. Her dad, who traveled often, would be regaled with play-by-play descriptions of Diana's participation, which were even more humorous because her mother didn't really understand basketball or volleyball and usually played up Diana's importance, rather than the success of the team.

"Philip, Diana just played like a pro today, dear. She just took over."

It wasn't true, and Diana knew it. It was, however, a sign of her mother's devotion to her. Diana was sure she was nothing like the daughter her mother had expected, yet she was the daughter she loved.

Tiffany's protestations interrupted her musings. "Diana? I just don't understand you. You can do better than him. Honestly, don't you ever look in a mirror? I wish I were as tall as you. You're statuesque! Plus, you've got gorgeous eyes!"

Well, if Mark would look my way, he would get a full-on view of my gorgeous eyes. She wasn't leaving until they made eye contact.

Diana—the huntress—was on the hunt!

Mark's real name was Roger. He didn't know why he'd agreed to go out with Scott and Javier. He would much rather be sitting at home on his comfortable couch reading Stephen King with his Jack Russell Terrier, Cujo.

"Come on. Just the three of us. Like old times. It'd be like a mini high school reunion!" Scott cajoled, gently punching Roger's arm.

Javier tried a different tactic. "You gotta get out, man. I know this bar that is filled with foxes."

Roger hated the bar scene. It was not a successful place for an average guy. He was uncomfortable with the meat market mentality. Scott and Javier were sirloin steaks, and he was "reduced for quick sale". All the women wanted hunks or movie star looks. He knew his limitations and was content with them in the normal routine of his life. Coming to a bar like this was outside of his comfort zone. He knew he didn't fit in.

So, Roger was more than a bit confused when he first saw the woman across the way staring at him. Although he had not directly looked at her, he had seen her as he turned his head toward Javier. She was way above his expectations. Tall and slender, she couldn't seem to take her eyes off him. He, in turn, couldn't look at her. Instead, he swirled his glass beer stein in his hand, watching the white foam evaporate, and stole glances. And every time he turned his head, his disbelief grew. She *was* looking at him.

It was Javier who first noticed the woman while scanning the room. He nudged Roger in his side. "Hey, you've got an admirer! Go over there and buy her a drink!"

"She has a drink," Roger growled. "And she's not an admirer. She probably left her contacts out and can't see two feet in front of her."

"So, just stay two feet away from her, and you've got a chance!" Javier laughed and exchanged looks with Scott, who snickered into his beer.

Very funny, Javier. She probably can't see you either; you're two feet shorter than she is, Roger thought, ignoring Javier, who turned to talk to Scott.

It always amazed him that they remained friends. When Javier first appeared in Roger's high school geometry class, the guy couldn't put three words of English together. Feeling pity, Roger offered to help him, and they had been friends ever since. Scott was a different story. Scott had been fat as a child. Roger, always sympathetic for the underdog, befriended Scott. To Scott's credit, as he grew into the jock status and out of his baby fat, he remained Roger's friend. Roger did not fit into any of the undesirable groups on campus, so he moved freely through school—tolerated at parties as Scott's friend.

Aside from befriending the needy, Roger did not make friends easily and learned to be alone and not be lonely. That philosophy had worked up until recently. At thirty-two, he was beginning to want a soulmate. He dated sporadically, never having more than two or three dates with one person. It wasn't that he was dumped; it was more that he dumped himself. He never felt comfortable around a woman, so even if things seemed to be going relatively well, he would eventually not call her for another date.

This girl, however, interested him. Although she seemed to brazenly stare at him, there was a hint of uncertainty in her posture, in the way her forefinger drew circles in the condensation on her glass. He liked her look too. He didn't want a little kewpie doll. He always felt oafish around small women. He wanted an equal partnership, and somehow, being physically equal in size seemed to be a part of that equation. Slowly, his forefinger began to mimic hers, making circles on his beer stein.

He's copying me! Diana was mystified. If he wasn't looking at her, how could he know she was drawing circles on her glass? She looked intently at his face. His eyes were partially hidden behind his glasses. He seemed to be watching his finger go around and around. Maybe it was just a coincidence. She moved her finger up and down. He moved his finger up and down. She stopped. He stopped.

Now what?

She had never been put in this position before. No, that was wrong—she had never *put* herself in this position before. Was she the huntress or the hunted?

Roger was starting to enjoy himself until he realized he didn't know what to do next. He had never picked up a girl at a bar. He met his previous dates through friends or at work. Should he approach her? Wait for her to approach him? What would he say? More importantly, what would she say?

Scott looked at his watch and abruptly stood up, almost tipping the bar stool over. "Man, let's go. Ain't nothing happening here, and I've got an open house tomorrow morning—big bucks for me if it goes for the asking price." He worked in his father's realty firm and talked a good game. But he lived in a one-bedroom apartment. Somehow, Roger didn't think Scott was making the "big bucks".

"You go, amigo. I'm just about to make my move." Gracefully, sliding off the bar stool, Javier headed toward a brunette with an eyebrow piercing and purple streaks in her short, raven-black hair.

Roger was beginning to panic. Should he stay or go? How he wished he were smooth like Javier or confident like Scott.

Diana watched the group across the way with growing alarm. The little god was on the attack, and the football player was smacking Mark on the back in preparation to leave. What if he left? Should she follow? *Oh, God, no!* He hadn't even looked at her once. She could just be imagining the finger dance they had been doing. She could make a royal fool of herself by approaching a guy who didn't even know she existed.

Look at me, dammit, she willed him.

And he did. Not just a glance—it was a full-on look.

Did he just nod? Was he smiling—just a little? Diana unconsciously nodded a bit, too unsure to fully acknowledge the connection.

He paid his bill. He looked her straight in the eyes, got up, and left.

Diana was stunned, then annoyed. Quickly, she slapped a ten-dollar bill on the bar. Bidding Tiffany goodbye, she hurried out.

Diana the huntress she was, and Diana the huntress she would be.

She had invested good staring time into this guy, and she was not about to go home empty-handed. She tore out of the bar and strode into the night in search of her prey. He looked like a downtown guy. She turned left and smacked right into the guy's back, propelling him forward into the FedEx drop box at the curb. Probably assuming some drunk had just assaulted him, he spun around to face his adversary.

Feeling both scared and impressed by the forcefulness of his expression, Diana stepped backward. Her arms stretched outward toward him, palms up, in a mixed gesture of apology and self-protection. Her heel suddenly caught in a sidewalk crack, and she started to fall. Roger instinctively reached out, grabbing both of her upraised arms and pulling her toward him.

Roger later would say he didn't know why he did it. He just felt compelled to do it. Diana claimed it was her mystical feminine powers. He claimed it was pure fear—fear of doing nothing one more time. They both agreed. It was an amazing kiss—the kind that lasts a lifetime. And it did.

Oedipus Wrecks

Sara Robbins was having a good day. No, it was better than that. She was having a great week! Standing in front of the antique, full-length mirror, she examined her new image.

"Stand up straight, Sara!" Her deceased mother's voice rang in her ears.

Sara rolled her shoulders backward and re-assessed. The suit was good—professional, a soft charcoal gray that showed confidence and yet wasn't stand-offish. She felt that confidence growing. She swept her hair up off her neck and into a French roll. If she couldn't be pretty, then this was the look she wanted—dignified, assertive, and knowledgeable.

"Smile, Sara. You're not pretty, you know. Fortunately, you have a nice smile, makes you look really pleasant."

Sara stared at her mother's photo on the dresser and grinned. She could do this. She *would* do this. Nothing could stop her.

It had been only a week since her ordinary existence had become extraordinary. As assistant librarian to the head librarian, she had been passed over for promotion time and time again. The current head librarian, Laurie, was a stunning brunette, eight years her junior with less than ten years' experience. Sara had been working in the museum's archives for twenty-two years. She knew every aspect of the job and often found herself tutoring Laurie. Even so, it was Laurie whose name was usually on the invitations to speak at any events. Sara ended up holding down the fort while Laurie's star power rose.

This time was different. Sara had developed a system of storing and cataloging art that simplified the retrieval of materials significantly. Laurie knew the system, but Sara had developed it, and so it was Sara who got the invitation to present the system at the National Art Librarians conference in Sacramento. She would be the keynote speaker tomorrow at the Friday night dinner.

She had to ask Laurie for permission to attend, even though all expenses for presenters were paid.

"Why, Sara! How exciting! Of course, you can go! I'm sure you'll do us proud!"

Was Sara mistaken, or had Laurie clenched her jaw?

The phone rang. Sara had few friends, and those she did have would expect her to be at work today. She knew her euphoria was over. Sighing, she turned from her open closet. Her eyes swept past the brand-new, empty suitcase and rested on the phone.

Maybe she could just ignore it, just this one time. Maybe it wasn't who she thought it was.

She knew better—oh yes! *This is your life, Sara Robbins. And your life does not include accolades and happiness. Your life includes your father, Sam Robbins.*

Sara plopped down on the bed and reached angrily for the phone.

"Yes?" she queried and moaned inwardly when the person on the line spoke. It was Edith, who manned the reception desk at Sam's retirement home.

"Hello, Edith."

"Really?"

"Is he all right?"

She listened, her euphoria evaporating. "No, I understand. I'll be there shortly."

Sara Robbins, the only child of Samuel H. Robbins, collapsed backward onto the bed, flung her hands over her head, and stared at the ceiling. Maybe it was just a little accident. There was little point in packing. She'd have to deal with this minor glitch first.

Once she had a life of her own, such as it was. She made the dutiful phone call once a week upstate to her parents, and her responsibility was fulfilled. First, her mother died. Then Sam got sick.

Sara vividly remembered the day she got the phone call from a neighbor. Sam had fainted on his evening walk. Had it happened ten minutes later, she would have made it to the Christmas Bash at the art museum. Ten minutes later, she would have had a night of memories to sustain her through the week of hell that followed. Instead, she spent a week sitting in a hospital room, wondering if Neil Woodman in acquisitions would have finally made his move. She had longed for that night. She had geared up to make the first move if Neil hadn't by 11 p.m. She had stood in front of the mirror, practicing her pickup line.

The triple bypass ended up being an astounding success for a man of seventy-nine. Sara settled her father back in his little bungalow, hired a housekeeper, set up nursing care, and ran back to her apartment. She had lost Christmas and New Year's. Little did she know at that time that her losses had just begun.

Sara dialed work and entered Laurie's extension at the prompt.

"Hello, Laurie Traynor speaking." Sara pictured Laurie: perfect posture, leaning forward from the waist, elbows perched on the edge of the massive rosewood desk.

"Hi, Laurie. It's Sara." Sara cursed her high-pitched, rapid-fire delivery.

"Speak slower, Sara. You sound like a chirping sparrow."

"Something came up with my dad. I won't be able to get to the conference in time for my award. My plane leaves at three, and I doubt I'll be done in time to go."

"Oh, I'm so sorry, Sara. Is it serious?"

To Sara, the tone was a bit too concerned—disingenuous, perhaps. She ignored the question. "Will you be able to go and present my paper? The PowerPoint is already at the conference. I needed to submit it by Monday. There's a paper copy on my desk." She was clenching her jaw.

"Of course, I can," Laurie replied as if she was doing Sara a favor. "And don't worry. I'll give credit where credit is due."

What does that mean? Sara thought. *Why not just say, I'll be sure to credit you? Who exactly did Laurie think should get the credit?* She realized she was acting paranoid. "Thank you."

"No problem. And I'm so sorry about your dad."

Sara hung up the phone. Laurie's last words rang in her ears. She could just picture Laurie dancing around her large office and mentally congratulating herself on her good luck. Sara slowly hung her beloved gray suit back on the hanger and pushed the new suitcase to the back of the closet. Changing into a pair of jeans and a sweatshirt, she headed out the door.

Sara threw her purse onto the passenger seat and started the car. She contemplated not having Laurie go in her place and just having the conference coordinator present her presentation. She held out on the hope that Laurie would give her credit; after all, Sara was listed in the program. She jammed the car into Drive, and the sensation of "life as usual" fell over her shoulders like a shroud of stones. She slumped forward under the weight.

Sara stared at the sour-pink stucco facade of the New Horizons Assisted Living Center and grimaced. Its large center door and the two cathedral-like windows above it made it look like a jack-o'-lantern. She swore it was sneering at her.

"Back so soon?" It seemed to be saying.

Sara pushed on the rectangular blue pad and surged forward as the large double doors floated inward. The interior was designed with good cheer in mind. Plastic ivy plants dangled from the tops of the plastic Grecian columns lining the walls of the entrance hall. The paisley carpet, which had most likely been selected to hide the spills and dirt, stretched all the way down the wide hallway to the reception desk. Undersized chairs with overstuffed cushions were lined up between the columns.

Seated on these chairs was an assortment of sleeping, staring, or vacantly smiling residents. This was the hall of waiting, in Sara's view. Meant for people who were no longer able to interact with each other, these residents spent their days watching and waiting. She wondered how they got there. The assortment of canes and walkers attested to their mobility, yet she had never seen anyone sit down or get up from these chairs.

Those residents who were still self-aware were elsewhere. Her father would be among them. He was disdainful of these denizens of the halls.

"I'm in the best shape of all the men here. They're all wrecks." He had flexed both arms, proudly displaying his biceps to the other residents who were unfortunate enough to witness this display.

Frankly, Sara mused, *he was right.* He would outlive them all. In fact, he would probably outlive her—she was sure of it.

Sara turned down the hall to the director's office. She had trod this path many times before. The director, Harold

69

Linker, "call me Harry, we're all family here," rose from his chair as she paused at the doorway.

"Ah, Sara," Harry greeted her.

She was quick to note his obsequious, concerned look.

"Edith told me she caught you at home. How fortunate!"

Depends on who's looking at it. "How's my father?"

"He's got a gash on the back of his head and a broken collar bone. We've got him confined to his room, and we're having the nurse check his pupils regularly for signs of concussion. Can't do anything for the shoulder. It's in a sling and will hopefully heal in time. He is a lucky man, you know. Most seventy-nine-year-olds can hardly walk, let alone run after tennis balls."

In all her forty-two years, Sara had never seen her father play tennis. She never recalled seeing him run. She couldn't disguise her sarcasm. "Apparently, he can't. After all, he fell, didn't he?"

"True enough." Harry agreed, realizing he should switch tactics. "We have given your father a good talking to, and I don't think he'll be visiting the tennis courts at the park again. He seems to be accepting. He does have choices here, you know. We can't forbid a resident from leaving the premises."

Nicely done, Harry. Took care of the liability issue right away.

"Well, I guess I'll drop in on him and see how he's doing." Sara turned to go but not before catching the slight shake of Harry's head. Sam's antics were even getting to cheerful Harry.

The elevator ride was a real thrill, pinned in by two white-haired ladies sporting aluminum walkers and smelling of talcum powder and feminine deodorant. They chatted animatedly about their exercise class. Sara smiled pleasantly. She marveled at how well put-together they were. She felt positively a slob as she glanced at their color-coordinated workout clothes.

She sidled past the two ladies' walkers and turned left down what seemed like the corridor to her own personal hell. Sam's door was ajar. An *I Love Lucy* rerun was playing. Luci and Desi's voices bellowed from the TV. She gently pushed open the door. Her father sat propped up in bed; a large white wad of bandages circling his head, a padded sling supporting his right arm. He seemed to be sleeping. Sara hesitated. She could leave. The staff would tell him that she had visited. Her job would be done. She turned, and Sam awoke.

"There you are, Sweetie! Thought I'd give you some excitement today. I know how boring being a librarian is."

There it was. The dig. Always never enough. Not smart enough. Not pretty enough. Job not good enough.

"Heard you were playing tennis?" she asked, the confusion in her voice apparent.

"Never too late to start a new sport, I say." Sam grinned. His bandages tilted down over his left eye, making him look like a drunken garden gnome.

71

"Apparently, it was."

Sam made a dismissive gesture and let his eyes wander back to the television.

She glanced at her watch. He seemed to be doing fine. It wasn't that late. If only she had packed her bag. Maybe she could have made it to the airport in time. Too late now. She wasn't going anywhere today or maybe ever.

"Hey, Sweetie." Isn't this nice? She rated higher than the commercial for McDonald's, even if lower than *I Love Lucy* reruns. "Let's do an outing on Sunday. You're not doing anything, right? No special guy for me to share you with?"

Subtle. No guy loves you, and you have no life. When Sam pried, he always followed with a dig. Or in this case, two.

"Okay, Dad. I can come get you at ten. We can have a picnic on the bluff."

He grunted assent. With the commercial over, his attention swung back to the TV.

Sara kissed him on his grizzled cheek, fixed his bandages, and left the room.

The elevator was filled with four women and one small man who cowered in the corner, overwhelmed by the assault of perfumes and high-pitched voices. Apparently, the afternoon movie had just ended, and it seemed there was disagreement among the women about what the ending meant. Did they get together, or didn't they? Complaints about the director's choice of leaving it open-ended were vociferously voiced by the largest of the women, leading to a consensus this was not fair to the audience.

The doors opened, allowing Sara to escape, her ears ringing and depression mounting.

The ride home was uneventful. No surprise there. Her life was uneventful. She could see it spread out before her, and it was not pretty. She knew it was wrong to think so, yet sometimes she wished Sam was dead or at least comatose. She needed to be free. She had spent her life trying to do and be what her parents had expected of her.

Free. What would that mean? What would she do differently?

She would travel. She was sure of that. She would join a choir—she loved to sing. She tried once, and her full-bodied alto had been a welcome addition to the predominantly female choir. She was kicked out after missing two performances due to Sam-related emergencies. The choir director had been blunt in a kindly sort of way. Since she had proved to be unreliable, they could not make an exception for her. Everyone had to commit; people relied on her. She said she understood. Turning in her songbook felt like she was surrendering her voice.

Sara couldn't sleep that night and the next. She wondered how the presentation had gone. She hadn't heard from Laurie. She expected either a text or an email saying all went well or even that it'd gone poorly—but no, nothing. *How disrespectful!* What had Sara expected? She was barely a speck in Laurie's universe. Sara could only remember Laurie talking to her when she needed her help. Laurie knew that

Sara was more qualified for the promotion. This made for an awkwardness between them. Sara's award was one more validation of her competence and Laurie's own shortcomings. Of course, Laurie wouldn't volunteer Sara any positive feedback. She would make Sara have to ask how it went.

It was about time she dealt with the Sam problem. He was ruining her life, and she was letting him. Her mind drifted to the bluffs. They were wild and rose straight up from the ocean. There were no guardrails. Someone could accidentally fall. She was shocked at what she was thinking. She needed to get some sleep. Her mind was going to dark places.

After a restless night of tossing and turning, she watched through her window as Sunday morning dawned bright and warm. It was picnic day with Dad. She dressed, carefully avoiding the mirror. She knew she looked like hell. She felt like hell. Gulping down coffee and tearing into a bagel she found shoved in the back corner of her refrigerator, she contemplated the day. It was a gorgeous day.

Great day for dying. Her or Sam? No, they would have a lovely picnic. If she was lucky, he would talk about current events or shenanigans at the home and not about her failings. She could not take criticism today. She was on edge: tired, disappointed, angry, and sad.

Sam, of course, was not ready. Sara sat in the entranceway waiting chairs, wondering if the ice pack would keep the deli sandwiches from spoiling. Finally, he came down, escorted by Edith, who firmly gripped his good arm.

His bandages had been replaced by a large gauze pad, which peeked out from under his Dodgers blue baseball cap. His arm was still in a sling, and he seemed to have trouble balancing.

"Here he is! The man of the hour!" Edith exclaimed. Her comment compounded Sara's resentment. She was supposed to be the "woman of the hour" and yet, once again, Sam dashed that honor.

Both Sam and Sara smiled wanly. She took her father's arm and led him out into the sunlight toward her aging yet reliable 2004 Honda Civic.

"Still driving this old Jap car, I see," Sam said.

Dig number one. Old car implied low pay. Low pay meant failing. So much in one short sentence. Well done, Sam.

The drive to the bluffs was a quiet one. This was good. No talking meant no ribbing. Getting from the car to the picnic tables was a slow and arduous task. The cooler filled with sandwiches and bottles of Dr. Brown's cream soda was on her left arm, her purse was over her left shoulder, and she was steadying Sam with her right arm. Tired and impatient, she could barely tolerate his slow progress across the uneven turf.

She busied herself setting out the lunch on the wooden, knife-etched picnic table. Sam turned his face to the sun, then he turned to look at his lunch. Peeling off the top slice of his roast beef sandwich, he glared disdainfully at the yellow mustard smeared on his rye. "Yellow mustard? What kind of

75

deli puts yellow mustard on roast beef? You know I only like brown mustard."

Sara groaned. She had remembered to have the rye bread toasted but forgotten to specify brown mustard. Failed again. "You're so right, Dad. That's the last time I use Lou's Delicatessen."

Sam grunted and proceeded to bite off large chunks of the sandwich. The offending yellow mustard oozed out the corners of his mouth. Sara ate and avoided watching him eat by staring at the ocean, which was just visible over the bluffs.

"You eat just like your mother, Sara. That's good, you know. She was as neat as a pin. She dressed nice too, like you do when you go to work. You remind me of her." He gazed into space, his eyes moist.

Sara was stunned. *Why now?* she wondered. *Why was he being nice to me now?*

"Your mama was a sweet, kind woman. Family first. You're just like her that way, Sara. Always there for me. Some of those poor shmiels at the home never have any visitors. I know I tease you. I really am proud of you. It's just my way."

She was overwhelmed with guilt and—yes—love. Sam had been a good father growing up. So, what if he was a bit demanding in his old age? She owed him, didn't she?

Her eyes were drawn to the activity at the end of the bluffs. A large group of pelicans congregated behind a makeshift fence. Squinting, she saw the sign on the fence read, "Pelican Nesting Area. Do Not Enter." Outside the fence, a lone pelican was nestled in the grass. One wing was splayed outward; it was damaged, probably broken. As she watched, a large pelican swooped over her head, carrying an impressive fish in its beak. As it approached, the wounded bird raised its head, squawked, and opened its beak. Arching downward, the large pelican dropped its catch into the waiting maw of the wounded pelican. Then, turning in a wide arc, it soared upward and back toward the ocean.

Sara was pensive. Her relationship with her father was just like these two pelicans. Her dad as the wounded bird, and she as his caretaker. "Let's go for a short stroll and work off those sandwiches. Okay, Dad?"

He nodded and, with her help, negotiated his way up off the bench. The path wound around the perimeter of the park and parallel to the bluffs. Leaving the picnic debris on the table, she held his good arm and guided him slowly down the gravel path. Feeling protective, she walked on the outside of the path, forming a barrier between him and the cliff's edge.

Seagulls circled above. Occasionally, a pelican would glide by and plunge into the ocean, emerging with a fish dangling from its beak. Up ahead, Sara could see them alternately land, flip the doomed fish into their gullet, tilt their heads back, and swallow. Some would stay to preen; most took off almost immediately to fish again. No other pelican approached their wounded compatriot.

The path was getting closer to the edge of the bluffs and the nesting area. To avoid disturbing the wounded pelican, Sara decided to turn around. Motioning to her dad to turn back, he started to shuffle his feet in a clockwise direction. She grabbed his elbow to steady him.

Sara didn't see the large bird coming.

Sam did. Letting out a hoarse yell, he ducked and stumbled, knocking into Sara, who found herself right in the path of the landing pelican. As she ducked, the gravel gave way beneath her sliding feet. Fortunately, she did not fall all the way down. Her descent over the bluffs was halted by a sharp rock outcropping. Unfortunately, that rock may have saved her life but not her mobility, hitting below her shoulder blades and severing her spine.

After two months convalescing, Sara finally had her breathing tube removed. She had only limited use of her arms and no feeling in her legs. Classified as one hundred percent disabled, she found herself in the convalescent home adjacent to Sam's assisted living. Her days consisted of physical therapy and the TV.

Sam visited daily, promptly at 10 a.m. The visits were painful with Sam alternately watching *Gun Smoke* reruns and mournfully staring at her during the commercial breaks. Conversation was sparse. After all, what was there to talk about? No one else visited.

Six months after the accident, Sam died. It was about the same time Sara's art cataloging method became widely adopted. Laurie traveled the country, instructing museums on its use. They called it The Moncleif System after the museum where Sara once worked. Her name appeared briefly in the Wikipedia article Laurie wrote—as a footnote.

Resurrection

Mary O'Hara Levin sat serenely in the bus terminal. Men in business suits and ties, women wearing uncomfortable heels and businesslike expressions, and tourists with backpacks and water bottles all swirled around her in purposeful motion, moving from one bus to the next.

Mary O'Hara Levin had no purpose and no destination, and that was why she was so serene.

For fifty-three years, she had followed the rules. Graduated high school, married her college sweetheart, worked the obligatory two years to establish her profession as a third-grade teacher, raised the required two children (one boy and one girl), and played the supportive wife and mother. Today, she was neither a mother, wife, nor working woman. She was a drifter by choice—her choice. What a novel idea.

Hal, her husband of thirty-seven years, had been a good man, a kind man. It had been his sudden death four months ago that set her on this journey.

His great joy was fishing. Looking forward to his impending retirement, he and Mary had been researching Airstream trailers, the old kind with the rounded, aluminum shell. They would buy a used one, and Mary would paint wildlife scenes on the cupboard doors. They would travel together from lake to stream and see the country. They perused maps and travel books she got from AAA, looking for campsites all over the country where he could fish, and she could sit on the riverbanks and sketch the scenery into their memory book.

They frequently drove the hour to the Kankakee River for some fly fishing. Every time Hal caught a fish, he would lift it up on the line, his arm fully extended, look toward Mary, and give her a thumbs up. She often dreamed of Hal holding his fishing rod next to her as she sat on the mossy bank. No words passed between them, just the warmth of years of companionship. She missed him terribly.

They watched National Geographic specials, taking notes, and discussing routes. It was while watching a special on the Grand Tetons that Hal suddenly went quiet. At first, thinking he had dozed off, Mary did not realize he was dead. Six months before his retirement, Hal died of a brain aneurysm. They had promised to see the country together. Although Hal couldn't come in person, he would come in spirit. This proved to be truer than she had imagined. She unconsciously picked places that had either a lake or a river. She would visit the water and sketch a memory in her sketchbook to share with him. She knew exactly what he would say. She could even hear his words as she sketched.

"You got those tree's roots just right. Like arms gathering water into its bosom."

"This one is a painting, for sure. Look at those colors, Mary. Those leaves."

"Is that me, down by the bend? Am I really that pudgy?"

This last thought made her smile. Hal had been a big man. Over the years, his girth had grown bigger, a fact that he regretted. Not enough though to pass on Mary's homemade apple pie or lasagna.

Mary was the complete opposite. She was a tall woman who kept her slender figure and, despite her fifty-three years, maintained the erect posture of the amateur ballet dancer of her youth. Were it not for the faint lines around her eyes and radiating from her lips, she could pass for a woman twenty years younger.

Mary was startled by the clatter of the schedule board as the lines of text flipped over to update the arrivals. She guessed Crossville, Tennessee did not subscribe to the modern digital displays of her hometown, Chicago, and the noise was somehow comforting.

She had been traveling for two weeks, choosing her destination by various games of chance. She got to Tulsa by picking a number between one and twenty and taking the fourteenth bus to leave the station. There, she had taken a daytrip down the Arkansas River and swam in one of its many lakes. Houston was chosen because the next woman to come into the bathroom wore red, red for Houston, yellow for San Diego, etc. She had stood on the bridge at Allen's Landing, watching all sorts of watercraft pass underneath. Crossville had been the old, traditional "close your eyes and point your finger" technique of her childhood. She hoped there was water nearby. She didn't want to disappoint Hal.

This bus station was rather small in comparison to the others. Staring out through the large windows revealed a narrow street with faded storefronts and anemic trees. Mary realized bus stations were often not situated in the best part of town. Yet here the streets looked clean, and the people on them seemed to move in a comfortable, unthreatened gait. Unlike Chicago, they neither glanced over their shoulders nor clutched their purses close to their chests.

Perhaps a walk was in order. Pulling her Samsonite wheelie behind her, she pushed through the large oak doors and into the sunlight. Sliding her sunglasses over her eyes, she glanced up and down the street. To the left, she could see a large, domed building about six blocks down. To the right, a church spire pierced the too blue sky.

Left, she decided. As a lapsed Catholic married to a Jew, she would pass on the church. She laughed. Her son, Scott, married a lovely Lutheran girl from Wisconsin. Hope was small, pale, and serious. It took her a long time to adjust to Hal's Jewish sarcasm. Try as he might, Scott could not get his father to tone it down. Hal's big concession was a wink in Hope's direction as a signal not to take *that* remark seriously. He winked often, and Hope gradually learned to smile appreciatively, even if it made no sense to her. Mary had hoped for grandchildren. Hope and Scott had been married for seven years and never brought up the topic. Mary wondered if Hope could have children.

She suspected Stephanie, her daughter, would never have children. She and her partner, Julie, had been together for ten years and even gotten married in New Hampshire last fall. Hal had feigned illness and not gone. She went. Happiness is personal, and although it was not her choice for her daughter, it was her daughter's choice. Julie was nice and loved Stephanie; that was clear. In retrospect, Stephanie's lifestyle had helped her decide to make this trip. If Stephanie could break out of society's expectations, so could she.

Out of her whole her family, Stephanie was the one who had tried her best to understand.

Understand what? That she had left everyone and everything to drift? That she hadn't even told them where she was going or what she was planning to do? Not that she even knew herself.

Mary walked with purpose toward the center of town. Scanning the storefronts, she returned greetings from complete strangers with a polite nod and a smile. She strode through the quaint downtown with a growing sense of calm and, surprisingly, belonging. The red brick buildings, the hitching posts (purely decorative, she assumed), and the slow flow of intermittent cars and farm trucks seemed so right. It was as if the town had a personality of congeniality in every inanimate object of its creation.

The end of the town came too quickly. Ahead stretched a two-lane highway that seemed to disappear into a forest of pines. Sighing, Mary reversed course. It was then that she saw it. Nestled behind the First National Bank of Tennessee was what seemed like an East Coast diner. Shiny aluminum siding swaddled a bullet shaped building with large rectangular windows. Several green and gold awnings were lowered halfway, shielding customers from the midday sun. The roof was adorned with a neon sign proclaiming in large letters, "Crossville Diner" and in smaller letters below, "Mama's Home Recipes Eaten Here".

Mary was suddenly thirsty—and hungry. Approaching the diner, she scanned the parking lot, which was half full. This was a good sign that the food was at least acceptable to the locals.

As she entered the diner, cool air caressed her. Scanning the room, fellow diners nodded silent hellos and returned to their meals. Selecting a stool at the counter, Mary watched appreciatively as a rotund, smiling waitress, with teased blond hair and a pink hair bow, moved swiftly from diner to diner, pouring coffee and expertly swiping plates filled with steaming food from the pass-through window onto counters and tables.

As Mary reached for the laminated menu propped in a wire holder, the waitress appeared. Mary noticed a matching pink name tag proclaiming, "Betty."

"Something to drink, darling? We got sweet tea, hot coffee, homemade lemonade, and, of course, most sodas you can think of. Me, personally, *love* that lemonade!"

Mary smiled. "Lemonade sounds great."

"Won't regret it, sweetheart. Back in a minute!" And she was down the counter before Mary's eyes could return to the menu.

Betty returned with the lemonade.

Mary pressed the cold, sweating glass to her lips. The sweet liquid caressed her parched throat.

Betty's round face filled with pleasure as Mary nodded her approval.

"Betty, that hits the spot. What's your lunch favorite?" Mary asked her.

"I wouldn't pass up Bert's chicken salad this time of day. Of course, if you're hungry, his fried chicken is the best in Tennessee."

Deferring to Betty's expertise, Mary ordered the chicken salad. It came with home baked corn bread and honey butter. She ate slowly, savoring each bite. After all, she had no schedule to meet. No shopping to do. No errands to run. No dinner to prepare. She sighed contentedly.

"Passing through?" Betty asked, eying the suitcase leaning against the end of the counter.

"Not sure yet." Mary surprised herself with the answer. Of course, she was passing through—but did she still want to?

"Couldn't pick a nicer town to park yourself in for a while," Betty said. "There's work to be done, rent is cheap, and the people are just the finest folk this side of the Mississippi."

Mary looked over her shoulder.

The diner was sparsely occupied. A lone man sat in a booth, sipping a beer, and reading the paper. Through the large windows, she admired the tree-lined street and quaint store signs.

"What type of work?" Mary found herself asking. Funds were running low, and she didn't want to dip into Hal's IRA if she could help it. Something about this town and its simplicity made the idea seem intriguing. She had lived her whole life in Chicago. She was a city girl who'd never experienced country living.

Maybe for a bit?

Betty pointed at the lone diner. "Charlie here is looking for a bookkeeper for his mill since his wife died last spring. You good with numbers?"

With that, Charlie rose from his booth, sauntered (he really did saunter) over to the counter, and held out his hand. "Name's Charlie, but you know that already." A warm smile etched deep laugh lines into his tan face. He was tall, lanky, and slightly stooped with a full head of gray hair and gray eyes to match. Mary guessed he was in his early sixties.

The negotiations went quickly. She would work mornings for him, doing the books. She would write invoices, purchase orders, and do billing. In the afternoon, she could run errands and would be done by three o'clock. She knew little of what was expected. She had only done some bookkeeping for her father's shoe repair shop when she was in high school. She also didn't know how long she'd be staying. When she told Charlie her shortcomings, he shrugged, saying she surely knew more than he. She couldn't make more of a mess than he had since his wife passed on, and any help for however long would be "greatly appreciated, Ma'am."

Betty suggested Miss Flora's boarding house. "Just one block down and to the left." Mary suppressed a laugh—it sounded so Old West and quaint. Betty called ahead, and Charlie helped wheel her case down to the red brick three-story house with a white wrap-around porch and ionic columns. It looked like a miniature plantation house to Mary. Tipping the rim of his Stetson hat, Charlie reversed course and sauntered back down the street toward the diner. Mary smiled at his receding figure. He looked straight out of an old western, cowboy hat and all.

The woman who answered the door did not look the part. A red flannel shirt and jeans adorned a sturdy, very tall, broad-figured woman who reminded Mary of a female Paul Bunyan. Mary was sure no boarder had ever given Miss Flora trouble. Except she wasn't Miss Flora. Her name was Lorna, and she was the manager of Miss Flora's boarding house. Behind her, a tiny woman of advanced years, sporting a pink shirtwaist with lace collar, sat serenely by the unlit fireplace, stroking a calico cat. Not surprisingly, this was Miss Flora. All was right with the world.

Mary's room on the second floor was neat and sparse. Lorna gave the tour and the list of dos and don'ts and left Mary to settle in. Mary lay on the bed and watched the afternoon sunlight fade. She was surprisingly content and unworried about tomorrow.

"Tonight, I must try that fried chicken."

She awoke the next morning sated and rested. The fried chicken had been exceptional. Although Momma, aka Burt, wouldn't reveal Momma's secret recipe, she could discern hints of red pepper and basil in the breading. Burt would neither confirm nor deny. Mary gave up.

Sipping a fresh mug of coffee between bites of French toast, Mary surveyed the early morning diners from her corner booth. The postman sat at the counter, chatting with a UPS driver. Four farmer types filled one booth, and two women in jeans and T-shirts proclaiming, "Buster's Tractor Sales and Repairs" were enjoying milkshakes while texting on their phones.

Mary grinned. Apparently, the women here knew their machinery!

She contemplated having a milkshake for breakfast tomorrow. She nixed the idea. She just could not justify all that sugar and fat having to be digested before 9 a.m. Maybe for lunch though.

It was easy to find the mill. It was less than a mile out of town. The Hatchie River formed the northern boundary of the town. Carver's Mill used only waterpower and an added electrical boost when needed to grind the local wheat crop. All Mary had to do was turn left out of the diner and follow the road until it dipped down to the river. Charlie offered to pick her up, but she figured she needed to work off the fried chicken and corn bread. Besides, she would be sitting for most of the day. Apparently, it was unusual to see a woman walking toward the woods in the early morning. Several truck drivers offered her a ride in their pickups; she graciously declined.

Charlie greeted her warmly and pointed to the coffee maker. After a nod from Mary, he took a clean cup from a collection on the shelf and poured a fresh cup. The refrigerator had some milk left, and he offered it to her. She declined, appreciating his down-home hospitality. Closing the door, he explained that she could put her lunch there along with anything else she wanted to keep cold. If she wanted to purchase something, she could use the petty cash, and he'd lend her the truck, so she could go back and forth to town whenever needed.

He sheepishly showed her the business side of the office. The pile on the left was all bills. The pile on the right was comprised of contracts and receipts, and the pile on the floor—well, she didn't have to worry about that one just yet, he assured her.

Next stop—a tour of the mill. It was clear that he was proud of the mill. The machinery was polished, and the floors were spotless. The mill had just switched from processing soybeans and was not yet grinding the new harvest of winter wheat. Switching to grinding wheat, he explained, required the mill be clean so the flour was safe to eat and there was no cross-crop contamination. He introduced Mary to Ed and Mike. Ed, a small, wiry man of indeterminate age, oversaw the machinery. Mike, a big man with an impressive red beard to match his size, oversaw the stacking of grain bags near the chute so that they were ready to fill, cleaned the shelves, and swept the floor. Each day started with an inspection; Charlie explained. When he gave the all-clear, Ed and Mike would start the milling process. Charlie would check in the loads of farmers, write them a receipt, and then the grain would be dumped into a huge hopper for processing. It was amazing how orderly the process was when the office was so disorderly.

Mary set to work. The four file cabinets showed some promise. Someone had previously set up folders and some type of organizational system. She started by sorting the contracts by date and putting them in the appropriate farmer's folder. Once that was done, she removed the farmer's folders that had no recent contracts. She would have to ask Charlie about them. If they were no longer farming (or were perhaps deceased), she would put them in the inactive file, just in case they were needed for tax purposes. She wrote down post-it tabs on her list. She would use those to flag the folders with contracts for this season. Green would mean paid, yellow would mean owed, and red would mean overdue. She noticed some farmers still owed for last season in addition to the current season.

Ed went and grabbed sandwiches at the diner, and the four of them sat by the river on a hand-hewn picnic table. The men weren't talkers, and, although they were curious about Mary, they were content when she said she'd left her job in Chicago and planned to see the country until her money ran out. Yes. She'd liked Crossville well enough. It was so different from Chicago, so she'd decided to stay awhile and build up her savings.

Mike and Ed exchanged amused glances.

"I sure hope you stay awhile, Miss Mary. Charlie really needs some help."

"Don't worry, Mike. I will get this mill's paperwork in good shape before I go and will even find someone to take over. I promise." Mary had no idea how she would keep that promise. For now, it soothed their worried brows and set the mood right.

A daily routine fell into place in a surprisingly short period of time. Charlie insisted Mary use his late wife's car, so she compromised. She would walk to work in the morning. Take the car into town and back in the afternoon for errands and walk home at five o'clock. She loved her walk with all the spring flowers and grasses in bloom. She anticipated she would be on her way out of town before fall came, and it got too cold to walk. On rainy mornings, she would ride with Charlie from the diner—her only concession to the weather.

Charlie was a man of few words. Mary, being used to Hal's gregariousness, initially found the silence awkward. That soon passed, and she began to enjoy just knowing he was there without feeling the need to make small talk.

The office was coming along nicely. Her post-it tab technique simplified bill collection. Charlie was uncomfortable with dealing with delinquent accounts, and she found her teacher skills did her well in this endeavor. Ed said she literally "charmed the coins out of their pockets". Her approach always resulted in full or partial payments (with added apologies). For those who could not pay in full, she would set up a schedule of payments which were well within the farmer's ability to pay.

Mary found herself smiling as she climbed the porch steps each evening. Miss Flora's boarding house was a step back in time. On warm evenings, Miss Flora would be in her chair with a cat on her lap.

Lorna was usually doing some chore—chopping wood out back, washing windows, preparing dinner, or sweeping the porch clear of leaves. At about 8 p.m., she would take Miss Flora to bed. On pleasant evenings, Lorna would sit in one of the two carved oak rocking chairs on the porch and smoke a corn cob pipe.

Mary courteously asked Lorna if she could join her on the porch. She loved the smell of sweet tobacco that emanated from the pipe in clouds. Initially, Lorna was a woman of few words. That was okay with Mary. She enjoyed the quiet evening stillness, and the less conversation, the less she would have to reveal of herself. Not that she was ashamed of leaving Chicago and her children. She just felt most people wouldn't understand.

So, it came as a surprise when one evening, Lorna broke the silence with *the* question.

"You got any family back in Chicago?" she asked, taking small puffs on her pipe.

Mary was startled and decided to answer with as little detail as possible. "I have a grown son and daughter."
"No husband?"

"He died this past January." Mary hoped that would end the discussion, and it did in a surprising way.

"My husband—he died fifteen years ago. Got me a son too. Matt's over at Texas A&M. Gonna be a veterinarian."

Mary didn't know if she was more shocked that Lorna had been married or that she had raised a son who was going to veterinary school. Lorna had obviously done a good job. It seemed that the concept of nurturing didn't seem to fit with her imposing physical presence. Then again, Lorna took care of Miss Flora's every need and ran the boarding house with efficiency and care.

"How did you come to work for Miss Flora?"

"Well...my husband, Dan, worked as the stable manager at the dude ranch just east of town. It wasn't a good living, but we lived on the ranch, and we got by. I grew most of our vegetables and had me some nice fruit trees. I could barter what extra I grew for milk and cheese from Hurley's dairy farm and staples from Crasswell's grocery. Charlie always had some flour for us—extra, he'd tell us. Knowing him, he paid for it from the farmers who used his mill. Still, it wasn't enough. Once Dan died, we couldn't live on the ranch anymore. Miss Flora offered my son, Matt, and me room and board if I'd tend her garden and help with the housework. Miss Flora was more herself in the beginning. She's a bit dotty now but no real trouble. I'll stay with her long as she needs me. It's the least I can do for takin' us in. It's a good situation."

Mary nodded, and the peaceful silence resumed. She wondered what Lorna would do when Miss Flora died. If

Miss Flora had family, they would likely sell the house, and Lorna would be homeless again. She secretly wished Miss Flora a long life.

Before she knew it, the summer was over, and Mary was still in Crossville. She had become an accepted member of the community. Her odd habit of walking to the mill in the morning no longer seemed unusual. And she had a routine going. Every morning, she'd have breakfast at the diner. Betty packed a chicken salad sandwich with a to-go cup of coffee. A wave to Henry, the mailman, and a friendly nod to the old-timers who duffed their hats as she passed, and Mary was out the door. Lorna had taken to making dinner for three. Mary insisted her board be increased, and they agreed on twenty-five dollars more a week. Well worth it, for Lorna was a darn good country cook.

Initially, Stephanie sent weekly letters, asking her to come home. Gradually, the letters evolved into the "why-are-you-still-there?" genre. After all, whose mother lives in a boarding house when she has a lovely, high-rise apartment in Chicago overlooking the lake? Having no way to explain to Stephanie or herself what Mary found so appealing about Crossville, she put her foot down. Letters about Stephanie's life or her brother's life would be welcome. She was no longer going to engage in the attempt to justify her current choices. The frequency and length of Steph's letters diminished. When they came, there was little news to report from either Stephanie or—by extension—Scott, who relied on Stephanie to keep the correspondence up. Mary was saddened that Stephanie and Scott were falling into daily patterns that left no room or desire to explore new places or try new things like their parents had.

The soybean harvesting had finished by mid-July. The winter wheat would be planted in October and harvested in the spring. In the meantime, it was their opportunity to clean and repair equipment and settle in for winter.

The mill's office workload was also winding down. Once the final invoices were paid and filed, Mary felt she would no longer be needed. Was it time to move on? Did she want to? Charlie had been silent regarding her role at the mill during the coming winter, and she hadn't brought it up. Ed and Mike planned to go work the oil rigs off New Orleans. If she stayed, it would only be Charlie and herself.

Labor Day was celebrated with a good old country hoedown and potluck dinner. Mary filled her plate with down-home cookin' and scanned the clearing for a place to sit. Seeing Charlie sitting alone on a hay bale, she joined him, expecting to engage in companionable silence once again.

"You got family?" he asked, not looking up from his barbeque pork sandwich.

Mary was startled. He had never asked about her personal life.

Charlie, maybe sensing her discomfort, added, "No need to tell me, you know? Don't want to pry."

She warmed to his consideration. "I have a daughter and a son. Both married. Still no children. How about you?"

"I had me a wife and a daughter, but it's just me now."

95

Mary was silent. She knew his wife had died. No one had ever mentioned a daughter. "I can't imagine what it's like to lose both a daughter and wife. I am so sorry."

"Yep, so am I." He shifted slightly and looked straight at her. "Charlene was going places. We'd had her late in life. Alice and I tried for eight years, and then finally—there she was. Our miracle. She was a bright one too. She wanted to go to school in New York City. Wanted to be a fashion designer. We wanted her to stay at home and go to Tennessee State. She said she had to go to New York City. She'd been saving all her money from her part-time jobs and went and got a scholarship to some fancy school, that Fashion Institute of Technology. With her savings and what we'd saved for her, we had enough to find her a place to live with four other girls in Brooklyn. She was so happy."

He paused and turned away. His eyes seemed to glisten as he surveyed some of the families gathered around the picnic tables. Sensing his deepening sorrow, she placed her hand gently on his arm and let it rest there.

It was several minutes before he continued. "Alice went up there to help her move in last spring. Charlene got a summer job working at some fancy-dress manufacturer. Just doing odd jobs and the like. When Alice came back, she told me all about it. She was coming around to Charlene's way of thinking. Everyone in New York City seemed so sophisticated. Charlene bought a slick, black leather jacket with fancy stitching. Alice took photos. She missed Charlene terribly. Charlene sent Alice back with her flannel shirts—

she used to wear them almost all year round. Charlene didn't need them anymore. She was gonna be a genuine city girl.

"She would write about how she knew all about the subways—riding to and from her job in Manhattan from her apartment in Brooklyn. She was coming home for Christmas. One day, just after Thanksgiving, we got a call from the police. Charlene had been walking down the steps into the subway. She was carrying several shopping bags. Her purse was slung over her shoulder, and some lowlife tried to steal it. Charlene wouldn't let go. He pushed her down the stairs. Broke her neck. Just like that, she was gone…She should've let go."

Mary was stunned. Instinctively, her hand moved to grasp his. He shuttered. She slowly took her hand away.

Charlie continued, his eyes staring into the distance. "He killed Alice too. She couldn't get over it. Slept with Charlene's favorite flannel shirt on her pillow. I watched her disappear, and I couldn't help her. They say she had a heart attack that took her. I know better. She died of a broken heart—my Alice did…for sure."

Charlie had never spoken more than a few sentences to her. It was like the floodgates had opened. Maybe it was seeing all the intact, happy families that reminded him of what he had lost. Mary began to think about her own children. Had she taken for granted the idea that they would always be there? What if something happened to them? Would they think she didn't care because she had been so noncommutative? She vowed to write both her children that night and plan a visit soon.

Charlie drove her home from the picnic, his usual taciturn self once again. As she started to exit the truck, he stopped her with a hand on her shoulder. "Thanks for listening. Guess I had to get that off my chest."

"Thanks for confiding in me." She stepped down from the truck and closed the door. She stood there and watched the old Ford pickup head back up the road toward the forest.

She wrote her children that night. The letters were brief. She hoped she'd been able convey her interest in their lives and her concern for their welfare. She felt a compelling urge to have them back in her life.

She didn't know what to expect on Monday. It began like a normal workday. Charlie going in and out of the office with receipts and invoices. Mary making calls to suppliers and doing the billing. No mention was made of their time together at the picnic. At lunch, it was just the two of them sitting by the river. Ed and Mike had gone into town to pick up some needed hardware for the mill. At first, they sat in silence, enjoying the sounds of the water slapping the shore and rushing downriver.

Mary was the one who started the conversation. "I've been thinking that maybe I should go back to Chicago and see my kids. It's been a while."

Charlie turned and gave her a long look. She was taken aback by the intensity of his gaze. He picked up his root beer, took a long sip, and nodded in agreement. "Yep. Be a good time to go. Not too much going on here. Family's important."

"I figured I'd go the end of next week. I've written the kids to see if that works for them."

He nodded and stared into the distance. "You comin' back? I'm kinda gettin' used to having you around. I mean, keeping the books all neat and getting things done."

"Well, if you need me, I can come back. Maybe in a month or so."

He turned to face her and said in a low voice, "I need you. I need you, for sure." His gaze never left her face. Her eyes met his. He took her hand.

"I'll come back, Charlie," she whispered. She turned and gazed upstream.

Hal would have loved this river. Mary could see the silhouette of a man fly fishing just before the river's bend. The way he cast his line reminded her of Hal. The man's line bowed and shuttered. Leaning back, he jerked a large fish out of the water. He must have sensed he was being watched. Holding the fish on the line, he raised his hand above his head and gave a familiar thumbs up.

She smiled and returned the gesture. A warm sensation spread through her soul.

"Thanks, Hal."

Her Cup Runneth Over

Molly Steinberg wouldn't have made matzo ball soup if she knew she was going to die that day. But since that information was not forthcoming, she spent a pleasant morning shopping, chopping vegetables, boiling chicken, and dreaming of the accolades that would issue forth from her children and granddaughters as they sat down to Sabbath dinner that evening.

It was a monthly ritual that she always looked forward to. Her daughter, Samantha, lived too far away to join her every Sabbath, so they had agreed to this compromise—Sabbath dinner would be at Bubbie's the first Friday of every month. Her son lived nearby, but since the death of his father, their relationship had been strained. Now, Ben only saw Molly and the family at this scripted Sabbath dinner.

Molly sighed. It had been four years since Ira's death—long enough to take the rough edges off his memory. She preferred it that way. Remembering the good parts made justifying their forty-two years together easier. Samantha tacitly played along, even naming her second daughter Irina in his memory.

Ben saw it all as a cop out.

Ira was a piece of work. He had verbally abused her—calling her a fat cow, even though his football lineman's physique had long since been swallowed up by excess. He simmered with the threat of violence yet never struck. Not that he wasn't capable. Molly was sure of it. She took solace in knowing he feared she would leave him if he crossed that line. The reality was that he had feared being alone—with no one to control, no one to frighten.

Her husband had been an accountant at a national firm. He worked there for thirty years, sitting docilely behind his desk in a non-descript cubicle. He memorized football statistics so that he would be able to make small talk in the lunchroom. He rarely got to use it. He usually ate alone. Unbeknownst to him, his inner turmoil constantly radiated over his face—not a pleasant visage over a tuna fish sandwich.

He hadn't always been that way. Molly first met Ira at his father's tire shop, where she had been a receptionist. His short, compact body and assertive voice stood in sharp contrast to his father—the consummate salesman. As heir apparent to Mel's Tire and Brake shop, and being fresh from college with his accounting degree, he impressed her with his take-charge attitude and competency with numbers. They dated and married within a year. It wasn't until Mel's stroke that Ira's shortcomings became apparent; he couldn't sell. The coup de grâce was when a Goodyear opened a half mile down the street. Desperate to keep the business going, Ira started bullying customers—trying to guilt them into supporting the independent business. Two months after Ben was born, Mel's Tires and Brakes folded. Molly often wondered if Ira targeted Ben because his birth and the business's death felt somehow linked to him.

Ira had been merciless toward Ben. His teen years were explosive. Ben soon realized nothing he did would make Ira respect him. So, he gave up, doing everything possible to make Ira's disrespect well-earned. Ben had gone goth with all the lip piercings, dyed black hair, and dark eye makeup around his smoldering brown eyes. He appeared as a black shadow, entering and leaving the house at all hours. He spoke little and glared a lot.

He even got a tattoo. It was supposed to be a secret, but Molly knew. She had become suspicious after seeing the spots of blood on the back of his white T-shirt. He told Molly a friend had been pushed into his back and gotten a nosebleed. It was a credible story—Ben and his friends inspired wrath from their conformist contemporaries. Then she caught a glimpse of him one evening as he was getting ready to go out. He was shirtless, putting on deodorant in front of his mirror. The rattlesnake began at the base of his spine and spiraled upward with its head poised on his shoulder blade. The words *"Bite Me* in dark red danced along its length. As his arm moved up and down, the snake came to life, bobbing its head. She could almost hear the hiss.

Ben looked up, and their eyes met. She hurried down the hallway. They never spoke of it. Molly enjoyed the secret forged between them that Ira would never know. Sometimes, when Ira got up into Ben's face, she fantasized about the tattooed snake leaping off Ben's shoulder and ripping into Ira's face. Bite me, indeed.

Samantha had used a different approach. She tiptoed through her teens, using her female wiles to charm Ira when possible and using tears when that failed. Ira saw his mother's image in her, so for Samantha, life was tolerable. She joined every extracurricular activity at school, making sure to spend as little time as possible at home. To the outside world, she was a winner, an achiever. Only Molly understood she was motivated by fear, not success.

Molly was startled by the chime of the grandmother clock on the mantle. Five o'clock. The family was expected in a half hour. She sprang into action. She carried the challah bread, draped with a silk embroidered cloth, and the shiny silver Kiddush cup into the dining room. Her mother had brought the cup to this country sewn into her threadbare coat and had refused to sell it, even during the depression when their family often went without food. It was Molly's ritual to lovingly polish the cup each Friday before Sabbath.

"Molly, I saved this for you so you would always remember me at Sabbath."

Her two brothers received no mementos from their mother. Molly was the only daughter, and as such, it was her duty to keep the Sabbath. She cherished that cup. It was the only remnant of her mother's unconditional love she had left. She would give it to Samantha one day, and Samantha would eventually give it to one of her daughters. It was her mother's legacy—*her* legacy.

She was setting the Sabbath table when she first heard the noise. Her cat, Shadow, jumped off the windowsill and ran under the sofa—something the cat only did when she heard the door open. A survival instinct from the days of Ira, who, upon arriving home, would swipe at Shadow, dislodging her from wherever she sat.

Molly turned from where she was placing the Sabbath challah on the table, laying the bread knife on the pristine, hand-embroidered tablecloth. The knife was a gift from Ben. She'd often wondered if Ben hoped she would one day use it on Ira.

She turned around. There, in the doorway, stood a stranger. He was not much taller than she was—much less imposing than Ira. He stood up very straight, holding a gun that was pointed at her chest. Molly's eyes immediately jumped to the silver Kiddush cup, newly polished and gleaming in the afternoon light.

Her eyes darted back to the intruder. She folded her arms, drew herself up, and said—nothing.

He looked confused. He wore no mask. Since he didn't care if she saw his face, he was either stupid or he was going to kill her. It was getting late. What if the children came early? What was he waiting for? No way was she going to let him hurt her children!

He said nothing. Molly was getting annoyed. The robber's eyes darted around the room, bouncing back to Molly as if he expected her to lunge at him. She considered it; the gun caused her to pause. *All right*, she thought. *I'll play the part.*

"Who are you? What do you want?" she wailed, her arms flailing outward, feeling as if she was in the rerun of a bad detective show.

He threw a pillowcase on the floor and gestured toward the china cabinet, where the silver tea set from her wedding lay, still in its original plastic. At least he hadn't pointed to the Kiddush cup. She couldn't stand the tea set. Her Aunt Martha (that old witch) and Uncle Solomon (the family lush) had given it to her. She was convinced Aunt Martha gleefully envisioned her being condemned to a lifetime of polishing. For that reason, she had never removed the plastic wrapper. Now, this stupid man was releasing her from its tyranny. She smiled in victory, picked up the pillowcase (*how rude to throw it!*), and dumped in the tea set.

She pointed to other knickknacks and valuables in the china cabinet. Boy was he ever confused! He nodded at each suggestion, and she, almost cheerfully, divested herself of the meaningless, albeit somewhat valuable, artifacts. Into the pillowcase went her collection of silver thimbles and Ira's pewter beer steins with their boorish sayings from every town bar they would visit on their annual, one-week vacation to some fishing hole.

Molly didn't fish; she didn't even like fish. She felt that she and the fish had too much in common. Both were attached to Ira in a painful, life-destroying way. While eating them, she felt she was devouring her own soul.

Finally, the china cabinet, the corner table, and the silverware drawer lay bare. She wouldn't miss the silverware. The modern stainless set she bought last year was more her style.

The robber's dark, close-set eyes roamed around the room and settled on the gleaming Kiddush cup. He pointed.

She shook her head. Something about his eyes reminded her of Ira.

"Get the silver cup!"

Not a Jew, she noted. Any Jew would have known that was a Kiddush cup. The harshness of his voice reminded her of Ira. She picked up the Kiddush cup and folded her arms, hiding it in the crook of her arm.

The robber was not confused anymore. He had a purpose. That silver cup was his, and he was not going to let this tiny, pudgy, white-haired old hag stop him. This was his first robbery, and he wanted it to be memorable. He was not going to leave with the memory of backing down to this woman. He felt mean. He liked feeling mean. "You stupid old bitch!" He lunged for the cup.

Molly stepped back toward the table. The fake Persian rug shifted under the robber's feet, and he slipped forward. A moment of triumph! He was falling, and she was standing—she had bested him. The arrogant, stupid man!

Take that, Ira! For it was Ira she saw tumbling before her, even though she knew it couldn't be. She thought of Ben's knife, lying within reach. If she could reach it in time.

The gun discharged. Molly looked down. Blood spurted from her chest. Clutching the Kiddush cup, she fell onto her side. Molly lay crumpled on the rug, her blood pulsing into the cup. He hadn't taken it. She had won. Finally, she had won.

The robber was stunned. He stared into Molly's fading blue eyes. There was something there, something odd, something disconcerting—something joyous. Scrambling to his feet, he grabbed the pillowcase and ran from the apartment.

They buried Molly that Monday, next to Ira. In her hands, they placed the Kiddush cup, newly cleaned by the funeral home. Neither child could stand to touch it, filled as it had been with their mother's blood.

Ira would have loved the irony.

Revival

Angela Manetti stared ahead vacantly, wearing a look of distain. *This is just great! I am now the archetypical picture of the little old lady sitting on a park bench in the middle of the day.* She sat, staring at her old yet well-manicured hands resting on her large bag. *Too bad I don't have a bag of breadcrumbs and pigeons flocking around me to complete the picture.*

How could this have happened? For forty-five years, she had been the office manager of one of the most prestigious law firms in the city. Twelve subordinates respected and feared her. She coddled no one. She demanded excellence. She was indispensable. Yet, at seventy-two, after all that time, she had been summarily forced out by mandatory retirement.

She had given her life to the firm. She'd had no husband, no children, and no real friends. Not one colleague sought her out.

Her bitter musings were interrupted by a tapping on her arm. She jerked upright and found herself looking at a small boy who, with great consternation, was poking her. Did he think she was dead? Apparently so, for when she looked directly at him, his consternation turned to fear. He bolted back to his mother, who was sitting on the next bench, rocking a stroller back and forth with her foot, and reading.

Great! Now, I'm the scary old lady sitting on the park bench.

The mother looked horrified. "I'm so sorry! Did Danny bother you?"

Angela replied as she plastered a mask of kindness on her face. "Not at all. It's perfectly fine."

Angela did not really find it fine. She found it annoying. What well-behaved child goes around poking strangers whenever they want? However, she had to applaud her performance as the kind, old lady. She learned to feign concern, appreciation, and gratefulness at her job. It had served her well.

She had almost given in to her true feelings at her retirement party. They'd given her a gold bracelet and celebrated her departure with an overly large, buttercream iced sheet cake with "Congrats Angela!" written on it in bold purple letters. The bracelet was nice, not that she would have any occasion to wear it now. But the cake was insulting.

For years, she refused cream in her coffee and cream-filled pastries, always explaining she was lactose intolerant. Yet, it made no impression on Natalie, the receptionist, whose job it was to handle retirement parties. Nor on Muriel, in accounting, who approved the purchase order. Muriel, her Wednesday lunch partner, who *knew* Angela requested no cheese on her meatball sub and rejected a piece of Muriel's custard donut when she offered. Muriel, her "work friend," from whom she'd heard not a peep.

So, Angela had three choices: don't eat the cake; take a Lactaid pill, which she'd had in her purse for who knows how long; or eat the cake and leave a lasting, pungent impression on her coworkers. This last choice was attractive; it would be a physical manifestation of what Angela thought of celebrating her retirement, and it would clear the room, putting a swift end to the party. In the end though, she took the polite route. She accepted a piece of cake and ate between the icing, feigning pleasure.

She was pulled from her musings by the mother's intrusive chatter.

"How I envy you! I haven't a spare moment of my own since the baby was born. Danny runs me ragged, and the baby is a terrible sleeper. She's up all night and sleeps during the day at the worst times. Like now! By the way, my name's Marion. I'm sorry. I'm babbling."

Angela had little sympathy for the woman. You make choices, and then you live and die by them. Her life had been serene, and she never had bouts of loneliness—until now. Retirement was like a slow death. She nodded sympathetically at Marion, feeling nothing.

Marion's soliloquy was interrupted by Danny's insistent nagging. "Mommy, Mommy, Mommy! Can I go on the slide, please? Please, Mommy."

"Yes, Danny. Remember you must use the ladder. Do *not* climb up the side of the slide."

"Okay, Mommy!" He took off running.

The baby started to stir and whimper. Marion sighed and pulled a bottle from a giant diaper bag slung over the back of the stroller. She glanced over at Danny, who was predictably climbing up the outside of the slide.

"Danny, get down!"

Danny, startled by the sound of his mother's voice, lost his grip and tumbled backward, landing on his side. Marion, looking panicked, turned to Angela, who watched the scene unfold. She busied herself by pretending to search for something in her bag.

"Please, could you hold her bottle?" The baby bottle loomed large and ominous in Marion's hand.

Angela looked toward Marion. She saw no way out of this. After all, her being there just screamed "available with nothing to do." She relocated herself to the adjacent bench, took the bottle with an aura of confidence, which she did not feel, and plugged it in. The baby began sucking.

"Angie will be fine. Don't worry. She's a great eater!" Marion shouted over her shoulder as she sprinted over to Danny.

Angie? She was named Angela? Angela stared down at her namesake. Eyes half closed, the baby was totally absorbed in the task at hand.

So, little Angela, what life will you have? Will you make the same choices I made? She looked at Danny and wondered if this Angela would be estranged from her brother as she was from her sister. Would she have lots of friends and dates and...love?

Angela looked down. The baby was intently looking back. Horrified, Angela saw the baby push the empty bottle from her mouth. What to do now? With her hand on the baby's chest, she took the bottle in her other hand and shoved it into the outside pocket of the diaper bag. Looking across at the slide area, she saw Danny studiously examining a red patch on his elbow, while Marion appeared to be giving him a marathon lecture while brushing the wood chips out of his hair.

Just a few more minutes, and I'll be free! Suddenly, she felt the soft sensation of pressure on her index finger. She looked down at her hand. She saw the baby's tiny fingers wrapped around her finger. She looked up at the baby. Angie was smiling! Angela gave a tentative smile back. The baby cooed.

Marion returned with a tear-streaked Danny in tow. "She likes you!"

Angela was surprised to find she took pleasure in that remark. *Caring what a baby thought of you? How ridiculous! What is happening to me?* "Well, I'm sure she likes anyone who feeds her." Realizing her finger was still trapped, Angela gently removed Angie's fingers.

The baby followed her retreat with wide eyes.

"Not really. Trust me, I've never seen her do that with anyone besides me and my husband. I'm so sorry. I've got to take Danny home and clean up his elbow."

At this, Danny shoved his bloodied elbow up into Angela's face. She backed from the gruesome display with an appropriate look of surprise and horror. Danny giggled. Angela found this reaction surprisingly satisfying.

"Thanks so much. We come every Tuesday and Thursday at this time. I would love to visit with you if you're free. Gee, I feel like a fool. I didn't get your name," Marion babbled.

Angela didn't know how she felt about the invitation. Did Marion really want to see her again or was she just being polite to the nice, old lady? On the other hand, she had been surprised by the children's reactions. They seemed to like her. Maybe, just maybe, she would try it out for a while and see. "I'm Angela. I'll try to make it when my schedule permits." It was a stupid thing to say. She was sure the statement rang hollow.

Marion did not display any skepticism. Her pleasant face lit up. "Great! We'll look forward to it." As Marion pushed the stroller out of the park, Danny turned, smiled, and waved.

Angela waved back and surprisingly found a smile forming on her lips.

She reached into her large purse with a purpose she hadn't felt for weeks. Rummaging around its depths, she pulled out a well-worn, leather day planner and removed the pencil from the loop on its side. She flipped through pages of scribbled notations that ended abruptly, followed by her blank pages of retirement. She found the current week and began to write. Today is Tuesday. She licked her pencil and put it to the paper. "Park meeting 10 a.m." Wednesday—she paused. She scribbled, "Dry clean pickup." She needed to do grocery shopping. Another notation. She looked at the formally blank page and was pleased. Thursday—she paused.

Looks like she was free. Licking her pencil again, she wrote, "Park Meeting: Angela, Danny, and Marion" on the 10 a.m. line.

Looking around, she snapped the day planner close, inserted the pencil into its loop, and, with a grand gesture, deposited the book back into her purse. She rose from the bench, slung her bag over her shoulder, straightened her back, and—with great strides—made her way to the park entrance, scattering pigeons as she went.

Samson and Delilah

Meredith Crawford pulled the zipper up on her pale blue Patagonia sweatshirt and examined herself in the mirror. She gave a nod of approval. At eighty-two, she was still trim with a full head of bottle-blonde hair and—due to a recent facelift (her third)— had no wrinkles in residence. She applied a subtle, mauve lipstick. The reflection was satisfactory. Time for her and Samson's daily constitutional.

Samson was, by all impartial observers, the most mismatched and ugly dog that ever walked the earth. How different from the cute pup she rescued from a box of puppies offered by a little boy on Halstead Road. He was a mutt of unknown origins. It appeared that a brindle boxer head had been plopped onto the body of a dark brown dachshund. A rim of white fur even separated the two parts. His tail was short and skinny and way too long for his height. The short snout and even shorter legs on his long torso did not dampen his enthusiasm for the outing.

He could barely sit still to let Meredith attach the leash. He pulled with impatience as she locked the front door and pocketed the key. She stooped to pick up the newspaper and toss it onto the porch swing. There was time to read the obituaries later. Hordes of teenagers trudged past to the high school, backpacks bouncing on hunched shoulders. She cringed inwardly at the purposely torn jeans, mismatched dyed hair, and rambunctious goings on. They obviously had not had the elegant training of cotillion. She turned up the road and headed toward the trail.

The trail was a soft, dirt path that wound upward at a gentle slope and around a bend to an overlook. Each morning, Meredith would sit on the lone wooden bench and meditate. Samson, being too short to accomplish the jump onto the bench, contented himself with slipping underneath and pressing his warm body against her legs.

It was fall in California. The morning sun was bright, the slight chill in the air invigorating. A few trees dropped their leaves, but the colorful oranges, reds, and yellows of her childhood home in Stamford, Connecticut were noticeably absent. It was the only thing about the change in seasons she missed.

She continued up the hill toward her bench. Samson fell slightly behind as his little legs struggled to keep up with her fast pace. She turned the corner and stopped.

This was so wrong!

The bench, her bench, was occupied by the largest man she had ever encountered. Rolls of neck fat cascaded below his ring of wispy hair. The slats in the bench sagged under the weight concentrated in the large swelling of the man's stomach, which extended outward almost to his knees. Sitting next to him on the ground, head resting on his shoulder, and staring directly at her was a large Great Dane. Anger and disappointment raged up inside her.

Samson reacted to this tableau with much enthusiasm. His piercing bark alerted the man to their presence.

He turned and smiled. His face looked as if it had been planted onto a bigger head. Where the inner face ended, a roll of fat circled from his bald head to below his chin. His features seemed abnormally small and grouped too close together. Everything seemed out of proportion.

Meredith suppressed a gasp.

A massive hand, which previously been resting along the top of the beleaguered bench, waved, and motioned her to join him. She hoped her dismissive wave would be perceived as a friendly, "No, thank you."

It was at that moment that Samson decided to live up to his namesake. With supernatural strength, he wrenched the leash from her hand and ran toward the bench with his belly bouncing off the ground. In horror, Meredith watched as the giant dog lunged toward him.

The man, seeing her expression, gave a reassuring flick of his wrist. "Not to worry. Delilah's friendly."

Meredith had heard that before. This dog could easily fit Samson's whole head in her massive jaw. She shuddered. A Biblical end for Samson. Rendered headless by a dog named Delilah.

Delilah collapsed down on her belly and slid her head between her paws in a submissive gesture. Samson skidded to a halt in front of her and sniffed her snout. Plopping on his stomach, he proceeded to stick his pencil thin tongue in Delilah's ear.

Meredith was disgusted. "Samson, cut that out!"

Samson was apparently too grossly absorbed and continued licking. Delilah, eyes closed, reminded Meredith of the expression on the faces of the woman receiving massages at the local masseuse salon.

"Have a seat. Looks like you're going to be here awhile longer."

Meredith glanced at the man. Where exactly was she supposed to sit? His massive girth left little space for company.

The man seemed to read her thoughts. "They call me a two-seater on the airplane. Make me pay for the extra seat. I can make room for you though—you being so trim. Come on over and sit a piece. It's a lovely view."

He moved over and patted the bench. The wooden slats creaked and sagged. Rolls of fat protruded through the space between the wrought iron arm and the seat. Feeling trapped, Meredith complied. She squeezed next to him. Her hip sunk into a soft cushion of fat as his massive leg pressed against hers. She had not been this close to another human being— ever.

"Name's Bobby. Robert Ulysses Grant, originally from Milwaukee, Wisconsin. My parents loved American history. My sister's name is Mary Julia Grant—Julia Grant was Ulysses' wife, you see."

Meredith nodded politely.

"What's his name?"

"Samson."

Bobby burst into laughter; the bench creaked ominously. Meredith envisioned the headlines:

WOMAN CRUSHED BY LARGE MAN AT OVERLOOK RIDGE BENCH COLLAPSE.

Bobby pointed to the Great Dane. "Delilah, meet Samson. And you are?"

"Meredith Crawford. From Stamford, Connecticut."

"Heard that's a nice place. Hadn't been out of Wisconsin my whole life till I moved here. Health problems, you know. Doctor's orders. What brought you out here?"

So that was the way it was going to be. Silence was not an option. She pondered how to answer the question. "Job opportunity. I was—am an artist. I designed sets for regional theaters and was offered a job here with a big Hollywood studio. Got tired of the winters back east, so I thought I'd give it a go. Worked there for over thirty years."

Bobby nodded agreeably. The bench wobbled. Samson glanced up at the sound. Delilah took this opportunity to roll her massive head over, exposing her other ear. Samson sniffed the new target and gleefully dug in.

"I don't think I'll miss Milwaukee winters. I've been here two weeks and have just been soaking up the sun. I live down there in Sunset Gardens, the over fifty-five condos. Doc says I need to exercise and take more weight off. Bad cholesterol and blood pressure, you know."

That last comment floored Meredith. More weight off? She regretted the question as soon as she said it. "How big were you?"

"At my heaviest, five hundred and twenty-three. Just broke the four seventy-five barrier. You see, I set myself these goals. That was a tough one. Aiming for four fifty now. Doc says if I can get under three fifty, I'll be in the clear.

"Never was a skinny kid. They build them big in my family—widthwise, at least. I was the tallest boy in sixth grade and then—bam! Stopped growing. Got teased a lot in high school, 'til I got into wrestling. Low center of gravity and big weight was a good thing for a wrestler."

Meredith nodded. Boys had it easier. She'd hit puberty as a freshman and gained fifty pounds in a year. Eric Graeber—the class clown and an all-around dirtbag—gave her the nickname Meredith Mammoth. She'd plunged into exercise and diet and eventually became anorexic. Two years of therapy later, she had put those feelings of insecurity behind her. Now, she wasn't so sure.

Bobby was on a roll. "I did fine cabinetry. Life was good. Young, beautiful wife. Good business, good customers. One day, I fell down the stairs carrying an armoire. Broke my leg. Worst part was that I bruised my backbone bad and pinched a nerve in my neck. Laid up for three months. I tried to go back to work, but my neck was in too much pain. Took me too long to complete orders. Business dried up, and my wife left. And I—well—I just ate and drank. Gained almost two hundred pounds in a little over a year. Felt helpless. But I'm trying to change now."

Meredith's discomfort was rising. She looked at her watch, rose, and jerked on Samson's leash. Samson looked up. He wasn't finished yet and showed no intention of obeying. Meredith's next jerk almost lifted him off his stubby feet. Finally, admitting defeat, he abandoned Delilah and stood up. Delilah sat up and proceeded to let out a pathetic concert of high-pitched whines.

"Nice meeting you, Bobby."

"Same here, Meredith. It's been tough for me to make friends here, so thanks for listening. Do you come here every day?"

Lying occurred to Meredith, but she didn't see the use of it. He would know soon enough that she did indeed come here every day. She put on what she hoped was a friendly smile and nodded, turning toward the path while pulling a reluctant Samson behind her.

"Well, I hope to see you again, Meredith!"

The next morning, Meredith pondered whether to wait awhile before heading back to her favorite spot to avoid seeing Bobby again. *Ridiculous*, she chided herself. She had no idea how long he would be there. Should she disrupt her daily schedule for him? No. Wake, eat breakfast (tea, one slice toast with cottage cheese, and half a banana), walk, meditate, read the obits, and do the daily chore for that day. Her life was fine just as it was. She neither needed, nor wanted company—or so she'd convinced herself.

So it was that this unlikely pair began to have a daily rendezvous. Bobby was quite the storyteller. Apparently, there were plenty of humorous goings on in the over fifty-five set. Meredith found herself looking forward to the next sequel to what Bobby called, "Sunset Shenanigans." His stories were never unkind and were always entertaining. Whereas, she would have viewed the people in his stories with disdain for their foibles, he saw them as sympathetic characters with hopes and joys and—yes—quirks and oddities to enjoy. She began to realize how lonely she had become. Bobby slowly became her connection to the rest of the world. She found herself recounting his stories in her head as she went about her day. Often, she found herself smiling as she did so.

Every Friday, Bobby reported on his weight loss. Truthfully, Meredith didn't see much change, still she told him she could see the progress. He beamed at her approval, and she liked the feeling his happiness gave her.

It was well into the second month of their meetings when she noticed a subtle change. The bench seemed roomier, and she noticed that his chin—his real chin, not the double ones—had become more prominent.

One early winter day, Samson came running up the hill alone. Delilah stood in anticipation. Barking and agitated, Samson pounced on Bobby's legs, ignoring Delilah.

"What's up boy? Where's Meredith?"

Samson turned and started to run down the path. Stopping, he looked back at Bobby and barked. Delilah took off and joined Samson. Bobby craned his neck, ignoring the twinge of pain. Something was very wrong. He heaved himself off the bench and walked rapidly in Samson's direction.

Meredith was lying on the path, back arched and body shaking. It was an awful sight. He knelt beside her. Her eyes were wide with terror. He noticed her cell phone a few feet away and grabbed it. He punched in 9-1-1. "They'll come, don't you worry, Meredith."

Meredith's eyes closed.

He looked around. They were a good quarter mile from the road. The medics would have to park at the trailhead and climb up to Meredith. He shoved the phone into his flannel shirt pocket, reached down, and gently lifted her into his arms. It surprised him how light she was. It was even more surprising that he traversed the path to the street with no difficulty.

He reached the bottom of the trailhead, just as the ambulance pulled up. He laid Meredith on the stretcher and stood back as she was loaded into the van, followed quickly by two attendants. Samson was trying desperately to jump into the van. Bobby scooped him up. The doors closed, and they were gone.

Since her stroke, Meredith and Bobby have a new routine. At promptly eight thirty each morning, Bobby and Delilah come down the path to Meredith's door. Meredith waits with her attendant on the porch swing, her wheelchair beside her. Bobby lowers the wheelchair to the walkway. He grips her arm and firmly guides her down the porch steps and into the wheelchair. Her attendant follows, tucks a fuzzy, velour throw around her frail body, and then heads back into the house.

Samson and Delilah lead the procession up the trail to the overlook. Samson's five steps to Delilah's one. Bobby carefully lifts Meredith from her wheelchair and onto the park bench. Samson circles the overlook with Delilah following close behind. Bobby says Samson is "getting his mail" from both the wild and domestic visitors to the bluff, sniffing and leaving his mark. That job being completed, Samson returns to the bench and whines until Bobby lifts him up and, wiping his feet, deposits him onto Meredith's lap, placing her limp hand on Samson's back. Delilah sits next to Bobby, nuzzling her large head into his ample lap.

There they sit. Bobby tells stories, Meredith smiles crookedly at the punchlines, and occasionally wipes the corners of her mouth with the handkerchief she holds in her good hand. Sometimes, they just sit in companionable silence.

Two friends, two dogs, and a park bench.

A Time to Live, A Time to Die

The old woman awoke to the clattering of a breakfast tray being placed on the convalescent hospital table.

"Good morning, Sweetie! Brought you a nice, hot breakfast."

How nurse Maria could be so cheery at this ungodly hour mystified her.

Maria drew back the curtains, exposing a scenic view of the parking lot. "Wakey-wakey."

The old woman refused to open her eyes.

The sound of plastic tearing was followed by the clatter of plastic cutlery onto the tray. She felt warm hands shove a paper napkin under her chin—like putting on a baby's bib.

This was just another indignity. She was not a child. She opened her eyes and glared at the cheerful continence before her to no avail.

"Shall we start with some juice?"

"Not hungry."

Nurse Maria slipped a straw out of its paper wrapping and stabbed it into the sealed juice cup. Leaning over, she shoved the offending straw between the old woman's clenched lips. "Oh, dear. They forgot the honey for your tea. I'll be right back, Sweetie."

The old woman hated tea, almost as much as she hated honey. She said as much when she'd first arrived. The nutritionist dutifully wrote down "decaf coffee" on her intake form. And yet, it was always tea—a tepid, tasteless excuse for a hot beverage.

The orange juice was good. She placed the empty cup on the tray. Her hand—what had happened to her hand? She had always loved her long, graceful fingers, which had caressed the pipe organ at the United Methodist Church every Sunday for over thirty-eight years. She held her hands up to the sunlight. Blue veins trailed into red, swollen knuckles. Her pinkies curled, unable to straighten. Except for the offending, brown age spots, her formerly alabaster skin seemed almost transparent. Gingerly, feeling the warmth of the sun, she closed her eyes and moved her fingers, imagining she was in the church playing "Amazing Grace."

"Mom! What are you doing?"

Startled, the old woman turned back into the room, dropping her hands into her lap.

Her daughter, looking confused and alarmed, stood by her bed with a small girl beside her. The girl was smiling.

Not waiting for an answer, her daughter looked at the breakfast tray with distain. "That oatmeal looks nasty! I'll go see about getting you some toast and jelly. Mom, this is Barbara's daughter, Dina. She's your great granddaughter.

You stay here with Great Grandma. I need to see her doctor and get the toast, okay?"

"Okay, Nana."

The nurse returned with the honey, poured it into the tea, and walked out of the room in deep discussion with the daughter.

Dina leaned over the bed and whispered, "I know what you were doing."

The old woman turned to face the girl. She raised her eyebrows.

"You were playing invisible piano."

The old woman nodded solemnly.

"I can play invisible piano too."

"I'd like to see you play. What songs do you know?"

"I can play 'Mary had a Little Lamb.' My friend Rory taught me on a real piano." With that, Dina's hands began to play. Her little fingers pumped up and down on the bedsheets with great confidence as she sang softly.

"Wonderful. That's wonderful," the old woman rasped. Her voice unused to speaking.

Feeling encouraged, Dina said, "I also can play invisible guitar."

"Oh, I've always wanted to play invisible guitar."

Dina beamed. "I can teach you next time I come."

"I would like that very much."

"Dina, stop leaning on the bed," her daughter said. "Here's your toast. I got you grape jelly, Mom. Sorry it took so long. I told them to make some fresh toast." With a look of satisfaction, her daughter proceeded to rip open the jelly packet and furiously spread it onto the toast.

It was clear that having accomplished the toast acquisition, she had done her dutiful role as daughter and could now leave. She placed a firm hand on Dina's shoulder. "Time to go, Dina. Throw your Great Grandma a kiss."

Dina glanced at her curiously. Turning back to the old woman, she stretched to her full height, planted a warm, soft kiss on her cheek, and whispered, "Next time. Don't forget!"

"I won't forget, Dina."

They smiled conspiratorially.

"Mom, I'll be back on Wednesday to go over the test results with Dr. Holgarth."

"Can I come, Nana?"

While searching her purse for her keys, her grandmother muttered, "We'll see. I have to ask your mother."

Dina's face fell.

The old woman struggled to raise herself off the pillow. Her thin arms shook with the strain. "I want her to come. She must come!"

"Okay, Mom. I'll bring her. Calm yourself. Come on, Dina. It's time to go now." She ushered a smiling Dina from the room.

The old woman fell back onto her pillow. Closing her eyes, she turned toward the window. Her hands smoothed the sheet over her body. The warmth of the sun caressed her. Her mind wandered. She was back in the organ loft at church. Everything was as she remembered it. The polished mahogany paneling, the sun streaming through the stained-glass windows, the choir loft filled with white-robed congregants. Everything was as she remembered, except there was one difference—Dina stood in the front row of the choir.

The girl smiled, and her mouth formed the words, "It's our secret."

The old woman smiled back and nodded. She glanced down at the music before her and then looked back at the choir. Dina was no longer there. The old woman raised a hand, and the choir rose in unison. Her hands—graceful, youthful—lowered onto the keyboard, and the opening chord of "All Things Bright and Beautiful" rang out. She scanned the familiar faces of the singers—all long gone—a choir of angels. Their voices filled the church with wondrous sounds of praise. The music swelled within the old woman.

Was it her time? If not now, then soon. It would have to wait. Just a little bit longer now. Just until Dina taught her how to play an invisible guitar.

About the Author

Living for many years on the East Coast, Susan Helene moved to California, and earned a master's degree in mathematics and Computer Science, while raising her two daughters and a quartet of dogs. Having taught in many educational environments, she joined the faculty at Fullerton College to become the first and only woman Computer Science Department Coordinator for over twenty years. When not enjoying time spent with her family: her husband, her two daughters and four dogs of various size and questionable pedigree, she studied ceramics, where she learned the varied processes of wheel throwing, sculpting, and tile making. The exactitude of computer programming and the attention to process and detail in her chosen field of art helped hone her skills of observation.

It was after presenting "Her Cup Runneth Over" to a writer's workshop, that she felt encouraged to explore writing more seriously. Her short story, "The Sixty-First Day", was accepted for the eighth edition of Montana Mouthful, October 2020 issue. She is also the proud recipient of a Second Place Prize in the High Desert Branch- California Writers Club pandemic anthology contest. Her story, "The Rose", was published in their anthology: *Survival: Tales of Pandemic*, published in 2020.

About the Press

Unsolicited Press is rebellious much like the city it calls home: Portland, Oregon. Founded in 2012, the press supports emerging and award-winning writers by publishing a variety of literary and experimental books of poetry, creative nonfiction, fiction, and everything in between.

Learn more at unsolicitedpress.com.

Find us on twitter and Instagram: @unsolicitedp

Printed in the USA
CPSIA information can be obtained
at www.ICGtesting.com
JSHW081110090923
47971JS00005B/208